CREATIVE WOMAN MYSTERIES®

Dog Gone Shame

Susan Sleeman

Annie's®

AnniesFiction.com

Books in the Creative Woman Mysteries series

Library of Congress-in-Publication Data
Dog Gone Shame / by Susan Sleeman
p. cm.
I. Title
                        2013904571

AnniesFiction.com
(800) 282-6643
Creative Woman Mysteries®
Series Editor: Shari Lohner

10 11 12 13 14 | Printed in China | 9 8 7 6 5

— 1 —

"Who knew choosing a champion dog involved so much work?" Shannon McClain brushed her unruly red curls off her face and settled the last folding chair in place inside the tent set up in Main Street Park in downtown Apple Grove.

She stood back to admire her work while her good friend and the owner of Ultimutt Grooming, Kate Ellis, knelt on the tent's earthen floor, attaching row numbers to the chairs. Tomorrow morning, owners would prance their purebred dogs around the center ring in hopes of winning Best in Show in the first Apple Grove Dog Show and Pet Fair, an event that organizers hoped would turn into an annual affair.

A contented sigh slipped from Shannon's mouth as she strolled across the tent to Kate. Shannon loved helping her knitting group, the Purls of Hope, raise money for local charities. This time around, they were raising funds for the local animal shelter. Not that Shannon was familiar with animals—far from it—but Kate possessed ample knowledge to make the show a success.

As Shannon approached her friend, Kate's head popped up. "All finished?"

Shannon nodded. "And it's only eight o'clock."

"It can't be eight!" Kate's eyes filled with panic as her gaze flew to her watch. "Oh, no, it *is* eight. I'm in big trouble. I was supposed to walk Scarlet thirty minutes ago."

She leapt to her feet. As she did, her foot caught on a chair leg, collapsing the frame and thrusting it into a neighboring chair.

Shannon grabbed Kate's arm to steady her before she tumbled to the ground too. Tears formed in Kate's large brown eyes.

"Hey." Shannon smiled at her flustered friend. "Are you OK?"

Kate shook her head. "Millicent Downing has lectured me about being late for Scarlet's walk in the past. She says a champion dog like Scarlet needs to be kept on a strict schedule. Millicent's going to be livid when she finds out I didn't get to Scarlet on time." Kate shoved the cardboard numbers into Shannon's hands. "I need to go."

"I thought you told me Millicent left early this morning for her spa weekend." Shannon tapped the cards' edges to straighten them.

"She did."

"Then she won't know if you're a little bit late."

"Hah! Millicent knows everything. No doubt she'll call me on the carpet for it when she returns. What's worse, if she complains to other pet owners in town, it will cost me a lot of business." Kate chewed on her bottom lip, removing the last of her berry lip gloss. "I have to get over there right away."

"Do you want me to go with you?"

"No. You keep working on setup. I'll be fine." Kate grabbed her backpack from the large metal cart once filled with chairs and slipped a strap over her shoulder. "I'll be back in an hour, tops." She marched out of the tent, her long ponytail swinging.

Shannon straightened the chairs, then attached the remaining aisle numbers. After a quick check to ensure the tent was ready for the morning, she pushed the cart outside for storage. The rubber wheels squeaked as she hurried through Main Street Park. Across the street, the Paisley Craft Market & Artist Lofts—the business she'd inherited from her grandmother, Victoria Paisley—was the only building in a line of many quaint shops where lights burned inside. Her shop wasn't open for business, but work awaited inside for the remaining members of the Purls before they could head home for the night.

Three members of the group—Melanie, Betty, and Joyce—finished setting up tables nearby under the park's tall trees. The leaves above them whispered in the strong ocean breeze that brought with it a hint of cooler fall temperatures.

As Shannon parked the cart in a small storage area near the group, a couple who looked to be in their sixties strolled by, holding hands. As Shannon watched the man gaze down at his companion with affection, it wasn't the usual bitter longing that settled over her, but a welcome inner peace instead. Peace she'd longed for since the death of her husband, John, more than three years earlier. Maybe she'd finally turned the corner and was ready to move on and fully embrace life again. If her dear friend Coleen Douglas were with her instead of in Scotland, she'd sing out a hearty "Hallelujah!" and say it was about time—as would the other Purls who glanced down the path at the sound of her footsteps.

Shannon smiled at her friends. Betty Russo, the extremely social owner of The Apple Grove Inn, held a plastic tablecloth in her capable hands. Next to her stood Joyce Buchanan, whose platinum bob swung as she settled a cloth over a long table. Melanie Burkhart finished a sign and clicked the cap on her marker, her hair now falling in shoulder-length waves after her recent battle with breast cancer. They, along with Shannon and Kate, formed the small group of women who gathered each week at the craft market to knit and socialize.

"We saw Kate race out of here. Is anything wrong?" Betty asked as she spread the cloth over one of the tables set up for the next day's vendors.

Shannon took a corner of the cloth and helped press it in place. "She lost track of time and was late for walking Millicent Downing's dog. Kate thinks she'll be in trouble with Millicent when she finds out Scarlet's walk was thirty minutes overdue."

"She has plenty to worry about, if you ask me," Joyce said, slipping shiny clips on the table edges to keep the breeze from sending the cloth airborne. "Millicent has quite the reputation for being demanding."

Melanie nodded. "I'll say. Just the other day, she yelled at Elaina at The Flower Pot." Melanie heard plenty of gossip while working at her part-time jobs at The Flower Pot and Shannon's craft market. "Millicent claimed the flower arrangement she'd purchased didn't last as long as she expected. Even though she'd gotten her money's worth, Elaina gave her a full refund to keep her from bad-mouthing her business all over town."

Shannon hated to hear one of her fellow business owners had been mistreated. "I thought Millicent was wealthy. Is she hard up for money?"

Joyce snorted. "Not at all. Her oil tycoon husband died a few years ago. That's when she moved to Apple Grove and bought the priciest house on the market."

"She's not motivated by money then?" Shannon asked.

"No." Melanie ripped open another package. "She's motivated by mean."

"Now, Mel," Joyce chided her.

Melanie settled her hands on her hips. "Well, she *is* mean."

"But you don't have to say it." Joyce's lips narrowed into a flat line of disapproval.

"You're right. I'm sorry," Melanie said contritely. "I don't mean to speak ill of her, but I get tired of the Millicents of the world getting their way by keeping decent, hardworking people like Kate and Elaina under their thumb."

"Maybe we should change the subject," Betty suggested in her usual peacemaking tone.

Shannon couldn't agree more. "Where do we stand with the show's preparations?"

Betty ran her hands over a bright blue cloth, smoothing out wrinkles in the plastic. "Once we finish the tables, we need to price our sweaters, and then we can call it a night."

The Purls had been knitting doggie sweaters to donate to the cause for a month or so. They'd completed enough sweaters to fill the five large boxes stored inside the Paisley Craft Market. Wanting to carry on her grandmother's charitable ways, Shannon had provided the yarn at no cost and offered to store the sweaters at her shop.

"Then let's finish the tables and head over to the craft market so we can get home at a decent hour tonight." Betty stifled a yawn. As the oldest of the group, she often tired first, but Shannon suspected she really wanted to get home so she could dive into one of her favorite Jane Austen novels.

When they'd settled the last tablecloth in place and collected the plastic wrappers, Melanie slipped her arm around Joyce's shoulders. They led the group through the park where swaying Oregon pines towered over more wooden picnic tables. Miniature white lights twinkled from the trees and lit the park with a romantic hue.

At the curb, Shannon stopped to open the power box and flip the switch. The lights in the trees and the large white tent darkened, making the brightly lit public parking lot stand out.

Joyce tipped her head at the many motor homes and trailers parked in the lot. "We have a good turnout for the show already. I hope this place will be packed tomorrow."

Melanie smiled at Betty. "Your idea for the town to rent spaces in the lot for the dog owners to camp out was pure genius. The fees will raise a substantial amount of money."

"I don't know about genius," Betty laughed, "but it seemed like a logical idea."

"Well, I still say you're a genius," Melanie added. "I don't have any of the business savvy you possess. Makes sense that I'm the only one in the group who doesn't own a shop."

"I'm glad you don't own anything." Joyce smiled at Melanie. "You can give all of us advice from a customer's perspective."

Melanie rubbed her tummy with a sly grin. "I'm more than happy to give you advice about your baking *anytime* you need it."

"Then let's get going. I have a box of Joyce's famous cupcakes waiting for us at the shop," Shannon said. The thought of biting into one of Joyce's Pink Sprinkles Bakery creations made her mouth water. Picking up her pace, she crossed the street and unlocked the front door to the Paisley Craft Market & Artist Lofts. The first floor of the shop boasted supplies for every type of craft the locals could want to engage in, while the second floor held loft workshop studios for artists to rent. Her friends strolled past the craft supplies and into Espresso Yourself, the coffee shop area of the store, where the Purls met for their weekly knitting sessions. Store manager Essie Engleman had set out the boxes of dog sweaters and a stack of blank price tags for them to use before she closed for the night.

"Anyone want coffee or tea with their cupcakes?" Shannon tipped her head toward the long coffee bar.

"Coffee, please," Betty said as she sank into one of the buttery-soft leather chairs and rubbed her arthritis-riddled knee, "if you wouldn't mind getting it for me."

"Not at all."

"I'll help you," Joyce offered. "Did you want anything, Mel?"

Melanie shook her head and pulled a pile of tiny red sweaters out of a box.

Shannon stepped behind the counter, running her hand along the stone top. She still found it hard to believe she'd been so blessed by not only inheriting the craft market and her home, the Paisley mansion, but also seeing her dreams of adding a cozy coffee shop come to fruition. She pumped steaming black coffee into a mug for Joyce and put it on a tray.

Betty added sugar and cream, then nodded toward the window. "Isn't that Michael Stone's car?"

Shannon spun in time to see Michael unfold his long, lean body from his vehicle. He wore dark jeans and a light blue polo shirt that made his dark hair look jet-black under the streetlight. He stopped on the sidewalk and peered into the window before offering Shannon a tentative wave.

"Looks like someone's here to see you." Joyce gave Shannon a nudge toward the door.

"You don't know that."

"It's pretty obvious with the way he's staring at you."

Joyce was right. He'd fixed his cobalt blue eyes on Shannon, and she was powerless to look away. The Purls often teased her that Michael was interested in her romantically, but he hadn't said a word to make her believe that was true. Shannon suspected the Purls only wanted to play matchmaker. Michael had lost his wife ten years earlier when a criminal shot her in retaliation for a drug bust. No longer a police detective, Michael now co-owned Stone & McCrary Security Consultants. He'd helped Shannon solve a few local crimes since her arrival in town—and he'd saved her life more than once. They'd gotten to know each other quite well as a result ... as friends. Never had they talked about more.

Betty pointedly cleared her throat.

Shannon caught herself staring and felt the heat of a blush rise over her cheeks. "I'll go see what he wants."

Hoping to tame wild curls that the ocean humidity often sent awry, she ran a hand over her fiery red hair and stepped outside.

Michael walked toward her, his confident stride unusually tentative. "You're working late."

"We still have a lot left to do for tomorrow's show." Trying to get a read on his reason for being there at such an odd hour, she watched him for a moment. If he had a purpose for his visit, he hid it well. "Did you need something, Michael?"

He opened his mouth and started to form a word, then clamped his lips shut. Not being an indecisive man, his action surprised Shannon. She waited without speaking to see what he'd do next.

"There's something I wanted to talk to you about," he finally said. "It's ..." His voice drifted off, and he toed his shoe at a sidewalk crack.

Fearing he had bad news to share, Shannon stepped forward and touched his arm. "What is it?"

He eyed her for a long moment, then shook his head. "Never mind. It's nothing."

"But you—"

"Have to get going," he interrupted. "Will I see you here tomorrow?"

Confused by his behavior, she slowly nodded. "I'll be working from sunup to sundown."

"That'll be a long day."

She shrugged. "It's for a good cause."

"I'll be in town tomorrow. Is there anything I can do to help?"

"We have everything covered, but if something comes up, I'll give you a call."

"OK, see you later."

Bewildered, Shannon watched him walk away.

He was halfway to his car when he stopped abruptly and spun. "I have this thing for work," he said. "A dinner party we hold every year for our associates to say thank you for their hard work. Anyway, it can be awkward going alone to events like this, and I thought maybe you'd like to accompany me this year."

"Accompany you?" Shannon replied, stunned by the unexpected turn the conversation had taken.

"Yes … you know … go with me." An odd tenor filled his voice. He slowly strode toward her until he stood less than a foot away.

"Oh. Like on a …" She flapped her hands nervously in the air, searching for the word her mind *refused* to provide.

He took a step back. "If you'd rather not go, I completely understand."

She shook her head. "No—I mean, yes, I'd like to go."

"Yes?"

"*Yes.*" She nodded for emphasis and willed her arms to stop fluttering about like the wings of a crazy chicken.

"Great. That's just great." He started backing toward his car, his expression a mixture of happiness and horror.

Shannon's mind raced. *What if his partner pressured him to bring someone along, and he asked me out of duty, all the while hoping I'd say no?*

"You're sure you want me to go?" she pressed.

"Yes, of course." The corners of his mouth lifted slightly. "That is, if you want to."

"I do," she answered without thinking. "When is the dinner?"

"Saturday at seven."

Shannon gulped. "Saturday—two days from now?"

"Is that problem?" he asked.

"Not at all."

"It's too short notice, isn't it?" He pulled a hand through his hair. "I shouldn't have waited so long. I didn't think about it until last week, and I figured we'd run into each other sooner. We can forget about it." With hands up as if in surrender, Michael began backing toward his car again.

She shot out a hand. "No, wait. I want to go."

"You do? Honestly?"

She did. She really did. More than she thought she'd want to. "Yes."

"OK then, I'll see you Saturday." With a boyish grin on his face, he turned to leave.

"But I thought you planned to attend the show tomorrow?"

"Right," he said quickly. "I'll see you tomorrow then." He hurried to his car, and, too stunned to move, she watched as he climbed in.

After he drove away, she closed her eyes for a moment, trying to imagine a night out with Michael, but shock wouldn't let her visualize it. *I'm going out with Michael. On a date! But is it really a date, or one of those events where everyone is obliged to bring someone with them to even out the numbers? Och! I forgot to ask where we're going.*

Her cellphone chimed in her pocket, pulling her out of her whirlwind thoughts. She dug it out, not at all surprised to see Kate's icon on the screen.

"Did you change your mind and decide you want me to

walk Scarlet with you?" Shannon asked, somewhat relieved to have a distraction.

Kate started sobbing and mumbled something Shannon couldn't understand.

Unease settled in Shannon's heart. "What happened? Was Millicent home? Did she fire you?"

"She ... she's here." A strangled cry tore from Kate.

Anger over the thought of Millicent mistreating her friend had Shannon fisting her free hand. "Do you need me come over there and talk to her?"

"No. Oh, no ... no, you can't talk to her." Kate's voice dropped to a whisper. "She's dead, Shannon. Someone killed her."

2

Shannon parked her truck behind Kate's car on the street in front of Millicent's house. She jumped out and started up the long, winding driveway. An earlier shower had left the concrete slippery and gleaming in the moonlight, forcing her to slow her pace.

A flash of movement next to Millicent's classic BMW parked near the garage in the drive caught Shannon's eye. Trying to get a better look, she squinted into the misty fog rolling in from the beach. The shadowy form darted across the front of Millicent's three-car garage.

Shannon's pulse sped up and adrenaline pumped through her veins. "Kate," she called out. "Is that you?"

Shrubbery rustled and the form took the unmistakable shape of a person before melting into the shadows.

The hairs on the back of Shannon's neck stood up. She shivered as indecision clouded her mind. Should she follow or would that be too dangerous? What about Kate?

Kate could be hurt. Shannon rushed to the house's side entrance, where Kate had instructed her to enter. She heard her friend's anguished sobs drift through the open door. Heart hammering in her chest, Shannon stepped over the threshold into a state-of-the-art kitchen.

"Kate!" Shannon called out and waited for her friend to answer. The only sound in the deathly still room was the hum of a large stainless steel refrigerator. "Kate! Please answer me. Are you hurt?"

Fear shooting through her body, Shannon searched the room for a weapon. She grabbed a rolling pin from an antique crock filled with utensils and crept across the tile floor as silently as possible. Holding her breath, she hefted the rolling pin high and swung around the corner.

Shannon's breath caught when she saw Millicent's body in the den. Dressed in capris, high-heeled sandals, and a bejeweled knit top, Millicent's lifeless form lay sprawled on the floor. Her unseeing eyes seemed to stare at the pool of blood surrounding her head.

Kate sat in a swivel chair hugging her knees to her chest, her back to the older woman.

"Och, no." The words slipped from Shannon's mouth, but her legs were frozen. She couldn't take another step.

Kate looked up at the sound, her face pale. "Thank goodness you're here," she whispered. "I found her like this."

"Have you called the police?"

Kate shook her head.

Feeling sick to her stomach, Shannon took a quick look around the room at the tall bookshelves, leather furniture, and the plethora of Scarlet's awards. A silver trophy in the shape of a large cup lay on the hardwood floor next to Millicent. One side of the cup was dented, and dried blood dulled the shiny metal.

Shannon took a few steps closer. "Is that one of Scarlet's trophies?"

Kate nodded. "From her Best in Show win a few months ago."

"What about Scarlet? Is she here?"

"Oh my gosh, I forgot all about her!" Kate looked around the room, then bent forward to check under the sofa. "She'd never leave Millicent. Do you think someone stole her?"

"Her cage is empty." Shannon crossed the room to the empty metal cage, looking for a clue.

"It's called a crate. Cages are for animals in the zoo."

"Right—well, her crate is empty." Shannon could hardly believe Kate cared about such a distinction at that moment. "We need to call the police."

Kate suddenly jumped up and hurried to the crate. Staring down, she pointed at the floor. "That's blood. What if Scarlet is hurt—or worse?"

Shannon set the rolling pin on the desk and squatted for a better look. "Based on such a tiny amount of blood, she couldn't be seriously hurt."

"This is a nightmare." Kate started to cry again and clasped a hand over her mouth as her body started shaking. "I should've run when I saw Millicent's car in the driveway and the door to the house open. But I figured she hadn't gone away after all and was inside waiting to yell at me for being late. I was so worried about losing her business that I wasn't thinking straight."

"Come on, sweetie. You need to sit down." Shannon took Kate's elbow and guided her friend to a chair in the kitchen where she wouldn't be able to see Millicent's body.

To clear her head and come up with a plan of action, Shannon took deep breaths of the salty sea air flowing in through the open doorway. Kate wrapped her arms around her middle and started rocking, her face devoid of expression.

Heaviness settled in Shannon's heart for her friend, and she wanted to get Kate out of the house as soon as possible. She dug her phone from her pocket and pressed speed dial for Chief Grayson at the Apple Grove Police Department. Having him on speed dial said a lot about her life since moving to Apple Grove from Scotland. She'd become the resident sleuth, solving various crimes that touched her friends and family—often before the police figured them out.

"Shannon," Chief Grayson answered, his tone light, "don't tell me you've happened upon yet another crime scene."

"Unfortunately, I have. Millicent Downing is dead." Shannon forced all emotion from her voice to keep from ramping up Kate's distress. "Kate Ellis found Millicent's body in the den when she came to walk Millicent's dog, Scarlet."

There was a short pause. "I see. And how do you fit in the picture?"

"Kate called me after she found Millicent." Shannon glanced at Kate, whose face was still devoid of color.

"I'm on my way," Grayson said. "Don't touch anything. You got that, Shannon? *Nothing.*"

"Got it."

"Is he coming?" Kate asked woodenly.

"Yes." Shannon slipped her phone into her pocket and knelt by her friend.

Kate folded her hands in her lap and stared down at them. "He's going to think I had a part in this."

"What?" Shannon blinked. "Why would he possibly think that?"

"Television cop shows always have the police suspecting the person who finds the body."

"You can't believe everything you see on television," Shannon assured her, though Michael had once said that finding a body automatically put a person on the suspect list until they could be ruled out.

Kate shook her head. "I appreciate that you're trying to make me feel better, but you know Grayson will latch onto me as his prime suspect the minute he walks into the room."

"He can't bring charges against you without evidence. And since you didn't kill Millicent, he won't find any. End of story."

"I suppose. But you know how headstrong he can be."

Do I ever, Shannon thought, taking Kate's hands and rubbing them to get the blood flowing again. "I won't let him railroad you. I promise."

"Does that mean you'll try to find the killer?"

"Oh, I don't know—"

"You're so good at solving mysteries, and I'm afraid this is somehow going to come back on me. Will you please help untangle this mess?"

Shannon sighed. The truth was, she'd discovered she rather enjoyed solving the mystery behind crimes. If her friend needed her, how could she say no?

"Of course I'll look into it," she answered, her mind whirling with things she needed to do before Grayson arrived and locked down the crime scene. "Can you wait by yourself while I take a quick look around the house?"

"Yes."

"I'll be right back." Knowing Grayson was probably less

than ten minutes away, Shannon hurried back to the den. The sight of Millicent's still body sent a shudder through her, and she almost backed out of the room. But Kate had asked for her help, and Shannon was determined not to let her friend down.

She pulled her focus away from Millicent to study the room.

Two overstuffed leather chairs and an end table sat near a large picture window. The far wall of the room boasted floor-to-ceiling bookshelves painted glossy white. The shelves held an assortment of dog books, trophies, ribbons, and decorative figurines. Several baskets filled with dog-related items sat on the floor. The room was clean and neatly organized. No surprise there, as Millicent had a reputation of being a fastidious woman.

Shannon used her cellphone to snap pictures of each item on the bookshelves and then crossed to a small desk in the corner and photographed everything lying on top. She took a few close-ups of Scarlet's crate, and then, careful not to touch the trophy, she squatted to take a closer look at it. Large scrolling letters spelled out "Wildwood Sassy Scarlet" in the polished silver.

"Hey, Kate," Shannon called out as she snapped pictures of the trophy. "What does 'Wildwood Sassy Scarlet' mean on this trophy?"

"It's Scarlet's full name."

"Odd choice."

"It's proper naming criteria for a purebred dog. Wildwood is the kennel where Scarlet was bred. Sassy's the mother's name."

In smaller letters below the name, Shannon spotted the date and the dog show name, Doggie Delights Canine Champions, held two months earlier. Shannon recognized the name Doggie Delights from the many commercials she'd seen on television since moving to Oregon. The company had a catchy jingle about their moist, meaty treats for dogs of all ages—the kind of tune that could get stuck in one's head for days.

As Shannon stood, she made one last sweep of the room. Confident she hadn't missed a clue, she turned toward the hallway just as red and blue lights flashed through the front window, casting a kaleidoscope of colors around the room.

The chief!

She rushed through the first floor and confirmed there was no sign of forced entry. Then she took a deep cleansing breath to calm herself before returning to the kitchen.

"Grayson's here," she told Kate. "I'll go outside and bring him up to speed. Maybe that will cut down on his questions to you."

"Thanks." A hint of color had returned to Kate's face.

Shannon stepped outside and waited as Grayson's police SUV jerked to a stop in the driveway. He hefted his body from behind the wheel and strode up the walkway. Wearing faded jeans, boots, a polo shirt, and ball cap, he looked more like a tourist frequenting their coastal town than the chief of police.

Sirens cut through the air, spiraling ever closer, and he turned to face the approaching ambulance. Blue lights twisting, the vehicle screeched to a stop in the driveway. Two medics jumped out. Shannon recognized one of them as Terrie, a cute blond girl who'd bandaged the rope burns on Shannon's wrists when Randy Parson had tried to abduct her.

"Why did you call an ambulance?" she asked Grayson.

He adjusted the wide bill of his cap. "Standard procedure. Where is she?"

"In the den," Shannon answered, assuming he meant Millicent and not Kate.

With a pudgy arm, he pressed Shannon out of the way for the medics running up the drive. "You'll find her in the den," he called after them.

"Shannon," Terrie greeted as she passed by.

Shannon nodded in response and then faced Grayson. "When I arrived, I think I saw someone leaving the property. I only caught sight of a shadow near the garage, but it looked like the form of a person. With the fog being so thick, I couldn't tell if it was a man or woman."

"But you're sure it was a person?" Grayson asked.

Shannon nodded. "At first I thought it might be Kate waiting for me, but when I called out, he or she ran off."

"Whoever it was is likely long gone by now, but I'll have the forensic team comb the area." Grayson started to walk away but then stopped and turned back. "Stay out here." He spun and strutted up the drive.

Not wanting to leave Kate alone for the chief's interrogation, Shannon trailed after him.

At the door, he paused and peered over his shoulder. "I told you to stay there."

"But Kate—"

He shook his head. "We've been through this before, Shannon. As a witness, you're not allowed to talk with Kate, or you might inadvertently change your story. *Stay here.*"

"I didn't actually witness anything."

He fixed her with a firm stare, and she shivered under his dark intensity.

"Fine." She clamped down on her lips to keep her temper in check before she said something she'd surely regret later.

Fortunately, Grayson's booming voice had a way of carrying, and after a few minutes, she heard him say, "We'll have to wait for the ME's official ruling, but it looks like we've got another murder on our hands."

Shannon had thought the same thing, and she suspected the medical examiner would agree. It seemed physically impossible for Millicent to slip, hit her head on the trophy, and then roll into the position Kate had found her in.

Wondering who might want Millicent dead, Shannon stepped away from the house and studied the grounds. She caught sight of Millicent's bright red BMW again. *Maybe the car holds a clue.*

She hurried across the driveway and noticed the driver's door was slightly ajar. Using the edge of her shirt, she covered her fingers and opened it wide. The warning chimes dinged and the interior light flashed on, illuminating the black leather interior. Millicent's keys dangled from the steering column on a ring boasting a large diamond fob. Based on all the talk around town about Millicent's money, Shannon had no doubt that the diamond was real. A designer handbag that cost a week of Shannon's income from the shop sat on the passenger seat.

Odd. From everything Shannon had heard, Millicent

didn't trust anyone. Surely she wouldn't leave her keys or purse unattended in the car unless she planned to come right back. Shannon glanced in the backseat and spotted a suitcase.

Had Millicent left for her weekend retreat at the spa, forgotten something in the house, and when she returned, surprised a burglar? If so, why hadn't he taken her purse and her car?

"Find anything interesting?" Michael's deep voice startled her from behind.

"Och!" Shannon jumped and hit her head on the doorframe. "You shouldn't sneak up on people like that."

"Sorry." He stood with his shoulders in a hard line, his jaw firm. The timid man she'd witnessed at her shop less than an hour earlier had completely disappeared.

To still the car's incessant beeping, Shannon adjusted the door, making sure it didn't latch and lock her out. "With the way you keep turning up at crime scenes, Grayson is going to start suspecting you of foul play," she joked, trying to divert his attention from her shameless snooping.

"I'll take my chances on that. Grayson knows I listen to my scanner to keep up with local law enforcement activities." In the hazy light, Michael's blue eyes looked black as night as his gaze pierced her. "I am surprised to see *you* here."

Shannon released a nervous breath. "After everything that's happened in the last few months, are you really?"

He responded with a lighthearted chuckle. "Since you put it that way, no, I'm not surprised to find you knee-deep in another crime. But I am shocked to find you at the murder scene so quickly."

"Kate called me right after you left the store."

Michael raised his brows. "Kate's involved in this?"

"She found Millicent's body when she came to walk Scarlet. It appears Millicent was hit on the head with one of Scarlet's trophies."

"And does Grayson know you're out here pawing through his victim's car?" His statement contained a strong suggestion of reproach, and Shannon didn't like it. Not one bit.

"For your information, I haven't touched a thing. I'm merely looking about."

"Ah. So the door fell open on its own, did it?" A hint of a smile crossed his face.

"OK, fine. One teensy little touch. But it was already ajar. I used my shirt to nudge it open further so I wouldn't leave any prints."

Michael's smile faded. "Tampering with a crime scene is a serious offense. Grayson would blow a gasket if he knew what you were up to."

At his apparent need to lecture her, Shannon felt her irritation rise. She planted a hand on her hip. "Did you have a particular reason for stopping by?"

"I thought I'd offer my services to Grayson," he replied innocently.

As a former police detective, Michael often consulted with the chief on local cases. He'd also helped Shannon in the past when her investigations turned problematic. *Tonight, he obviously wants to help Chief Grayson, not me.*

"Grayson's inside," she said, her voice flat.

"Then I'll leave you alone to continue *not* touching anything." Michael gave her a look of warning before turning away.

She opened her mouth to reply, but the medics came

strolling out of the house, their heads bent together, and she decided it would be a better use of her energy to listen to their conversation.

Seeming oblivious to her angst, Michael strolled up the sidewalk, nodding a greeting to the medics as he passed.

"You really think Kate killed her?" Terrie asked her partner as they passed Shannon.

The medic shrugged. "The body's still warm, so she hasn't been dead long. I guess that means Kate could have killed her." He shook his head. "But it's hard to believe someone I went to school with might be a murderer."

Shannon's mouth dropped open. *How could they possibly suspect Kate had anything to do with Millicent's death? Will the entire town think the same way?*

Surely not. Many of the townsfolk knew Kate well—had witnessed her generous nature. Kate always thought of others in the community, and the people who knew her would give her the benefit of the doubt.

Would Chief Grayson do the same?

— 3 —

Despite Michael's warning, Shannon finished her inspection of the car. Though less than optimal lighting existed in the vehicle, she snapped copious pictures with her cellphone. Satisfied she hadn't missed anything, she tucked her phone away and returned to the house to check on Kate.

Grayson's testy voice boomed though the doorway. The urge to join them was stronger than ever, but Shannon knew Grayson would not allow her in the room. Quietly, she tiptoed forward and leaned casually against the wall by the open door.

"Let's back up to your claim that Millicent had gone to the spa for the weekend," she heard Grayson say. "I thought she was all about dogs. Seems like she'd want to be here for the show."

"Scarlet recently won a prestigious national title, and Millicent said local competitions like ours were beneath Scarlet now." Kate paused. "Also, Millicent didn't get along with many of the dog owners registered for our show. She never actually said she didn't want to spend time with them, but anyone with an ounce of brains could tell that's what she thought."

"And what about you? How well did you get along with Millicent?"

Kate sighed. "About as well as anyone else. She was demanding and hard to please at times, so I worked hard to keep her business."

"Meaning you had some difficulties."

Shannon pushed off the wall and dared a peek inside the room. She saw Grayson cross his arms—never a good sign. He started to turn his head in her direction, and she jerked her head back.

"Millicent was a hard person to please," Kate said. "I need every client I can get, and that meant doing whatever she asked, even if I didn't always agree with it."

"Did she ask you to do something tonight that you didn't agree with?" Grayson's voice carried a dangerous edge.

"No. I was here to walk Scarlet, like I said before."

"And you claim Millicent was already dead when you arrived?"

"Yes!" Kate's voice rose. "You have to know I'd never hurt anyone."

"Whoa, calm down. You act as though I've accused you of something." He paused. "As though you have something to hide."

"I don't."

"Mm-hm. Is it possible you got tired of trying to please Millicent and let her know it tonight? Perhaps you all had an argument, and in the heat of the moment—"

"That's not what happened!"

Shannon couldn't stand to hear Grayson badger her friend any longer. She stepped into the kitchen and found Kate still sitting in the same chair. Grayson loomed over her with a notepad in his hand, his back to Shannon.

Michael leaned against the granite countertop off to the side, warning her with his eyes to keep quiet.

She ignored the warning. "You're bullying her," she said

to Grayson as she crossed the room to stand next to Kate.

Grayson met Shannon's accusing gaze with a frustrated one of his own. "You have to know by now that the person who finds a body is *always* a suspect until we can rule them out. That means Kate is on my list until further notice."

"We both know she didn't do it. Wouldn't you be better off focusing your energy on who stole the missing dog—and the other clues—instead of Kate?"

Grayson cocked an eyebrow. "Perhaps no one stole the dog. Kate said the door was open when she arrived. The dog could've run off."

Kate shook her head. "Scarlet is well trained. She wouldn't run away from Millicent any more than one of us would dare walk away from her."

Grayson eyed Kate. "Obviously Millicent's behavior affected you more than you've admitted."

She groaned. "I simply meant that Scarlet saw Millicent as her pack leader. If someone attacked Millicent, Scarlet would defend her if at all possible. Scarlet would not run away—someone took her."

"She's got a point, Grayson," Michael said from across the room. "I owned dogs growing up. They're fiercely loyal."

"There's blood on the floor by the dog crate," Shannon told the chief. "Maybe it belongs to the killer. If you collect a sample, perhaps it would lead you to him through DNA."

"I believe if we find Scarlet," Kate added, "we'll find the killer."

Grayson considered their comments. "I'm still not convinced that the mutt didn't run away, but I'll put out an alert for Scarlet." He turned to Kate. "I'll need a description."

Kate hissed out a stressful breath. "She's a purebred Havanese. All white. There are pictures of her in the den, but she looks different now. She retired after her win at the Doggie Delights show, and Millicent had me give Scarlet a puppy cut. I have pictures of her with the shorter cut at my shop if you want them."

Grayson nodded. "Drop them by the station as soon as you can." He turned to Shannon. "If you'll step outside with me for a moment, I'd like to ask you a couple of questions, and then the two of you can be on your way."

"Of course."

Grayson glanced at Michael. "I'd appreciate it if you'd stay with Kate while I talk to Shannon." Shannon knew Grayson wasn't asking Michael to remain in the house for Kate's well-being. He wanted to make sure Kate didn't touch anything.

"I'd be glad to help." Michael moved closer to Kate, his expression softening.

Outside, Shannon walked far enough from the house so Kate wouldn't overhear Grayson's thunderous voice. A crowd of neighbors had formed at the sidewalk. They chatted excitedly, but they were too far away for Shannon to make out their words. Grayson leaned down to his shoulder mic and requested an officer to keep them at bay. After a protracted warning look to the crowd, he turned his attention to Shannon.

"Before you start pummeling me with questions," she said preemptively, "I've already told you everything I know about Millicent's death."

"I want you to tell me exactly what you saw when you entered the house."

A swift ocean breeze sent a shiver over Shannon's body,

and she tugged her sweater tighter around her. "I stepped into the kitchen and heard Kate moaning in another room. I thought someone had hurt her, so I grabbed a rolling pin for defense and entered the den. I found Kate in a state of shock and sitting in a chair, her back to Millicent's body."

"Just as I thought." He watched her carefully. "For all you know, Kate could've hit Millicent with the trophy and then pretended to be in shock."

Shannon stared in disbelief. "Does she look like she's pretending? Kate would never do such a thing."

He lifted his cap and scratched his head. "How well did Kate and Millicent get along?"

"Kate, like nearly everyone else in town, I'm told, walked on eggshells around Millicent."

"Did they have any altercations that you know of?"

"No," Shannon said, but she couldn't help but think they *would* have had an argument if Millicent had lived long enough to learn that Kate was late for walking Scarlet.

"You're sure?"

Shannon shrugged nonchalantly. "I don't know everything that happened before I moved to Apple Grove, but since I've been here, I haven't heard of any issues."

Chief Grayson clamped a hand on his holstered weapon. "If you're keeping something from me because you're trying to protect Kate, you know I'll find out about it—and you could be charged with obstructing justice."

Shannon cleared her throat. "I've told you everything I know to be fact. If that's all, I'd like to take Kate home. She's very upset."

Grayson's focus didn't waver. "That's all for now."

Shannon hurried inside. She found Michael squatting next to Kate, his tone comforting and reassuring as he spoke to her.

Shannon smiled warmly at Kate. "Grayson says we can leave."

Kate sighed. "Thank goodness."

Michael stood. Over six feet tall, he towered above them both, but his gentle expression kept him from appearing intimidating. He offered Kate a hand and helped her to her feet. "Call me if you need anything."

Looking dazed, Kate stared up at him. "Thank you, but I hope this will all be over soon, and I won't need any help."

Shannon wished she shared Kate's optimism, but the investigation into Millicent's death hadn't even begun, and Kate was already under a cloud of suspicion. Shannon wrapped her arm around Kate and urged her toward the door.

Michael caught Shannon's eye. "That goes for you too, Shannon. Call me if you need anything."

She felt a little niggling of remorse over being terse with him earlier in the driveway. "Thank you. I appreciate the offer."

Outside, she found Grayson still standing in the same spot. He let his gaze run over both of them as they approached. Just as he opened his mouth to speak, Eloise White, an older, well-respected resident of Apple Grove, rushed up the drive and stabbed her finger in Kate's direction.

"You can't let her go," Eloise nearly shouted. "She's the killer!"

Kate paled beneath the woman's accusing glare.

"What's the meaning of this, Eloise?" Grayson asked calmly.

"Two days ago, I overheard Kate saying things about Millicent," Eloise said. "Suspicious things."

All eyes swung to Kate.

Kate's eyes widened. "I have no idea what she's talking about."

Eloise planted a hand on her hip. "Oh, I think you do. When you were grooming Scarlet, and I was with Buffy in the waiting area, I heard you saying things to Scarlet about how she deserved a better owner—someone who loved her for herself and not just because she was a prizewinning dog. You also said that if you had your way, you'd take Scarlet from Millicent and find her a good home."

Kate's face blanched. "I was just commiserating with Scarlet because Millicent had yelled at her for not being perfect. Millicent was always too harsh with Scarlet."

"So you admit to saying those things about Millicent?" Grayson focused on Kate.

"I may have, but—"

"And you finally reached your breaking point tonight," Grayson interrupted. "You planned to kidnap Scarlet, but Millicent caught you in the act."

"No!" Kate shouted, then she covered her face with her hands. "This can't be happening."

Grayson took a step closer to Kate. "It's a great explanation for why Scarlet's missing. *You* took her, and then you returned and called Shannon."

"She was missing when I got here, I swear." Kate lowered her hands. "I would never steal someone's dog, much less murder another human being."

"Not premeditated, perhaps." The chief rubbed his chin.

"But it's hard to believe you'd leave a dog in a less than desirable home when you're always working to save animals from bad situations. Especially after what Eloise just told us."

Kate focused on Shannon. Her pleading expression said she wanted Shannon to do something to help, but with Scarlet missing, and with Kate admitting she'd bad-mouthed Millicent, Shannon had nothing solid to offer to refute Grayson's claim.

"We'll talk again soon, Kate," Grayson continued. "Make sure you don't leave town without my knowledge."

Eloise's mouth dropped open. "You're letting her go?"

"Trust me, Eloise. She may be going home tonight, but I won't let this drop until I get to the bottom of it."

Shannon hugged Kate close and steered her away from Eloise. "You're in no condition to drive. I'll give you a ride."

"What about my car?" Kate asked.

"Give me your keys, and we'll have the Purls pick it up and drop it at your place."

Kate dug out her keys, and Shannon pocketed them. She shielded Kate from nosy neighbors as they walked to her truck, affectionately called "Old Blue." Shannon climbed in and turned the key. The engine on the 1955 Ford sputtered, then caught, and they soon chugged down the street in a puff of smoke.

Kate swiveled on the cream-and-aqua seat. "Do you think Grayson *honestly* believes I took Scarlet?"

Shannon thought for a moment. "He has no choice but to look into it, but it's hard to tell what he truly believes."

"Well, he certainly won't find her with me."

"That goes without saying."

Kate stared out the window then suddenly spun back toward Shannon. "Can you take me home before we go back to the park? I can't go down there looking like this."

Shannon shot Kate a surprised look. "I wasn't taking you to the park. We've finished setting up. After everything that's happened, I assumed you'd want to go home and stay there."

"I can't bail on tomorrow's preparations."

"The only thing left to do is price the sweaters in the boxes at my store, and we can handle that. The girls were already working on it when I left."

"I want to help." Kate's lips tightened in determination.

Shannon slowed at a stop sign and appraised her friend. "After all you've been through, are you sure you don't want to just go home? Perhaps make a cup of tea and regroup?"

"Positive," Kate said vehemently. "I'd prefer to be with my friends rather than sitting at home alone, stewing."

Shannon understood Kate's desire to surround herself with the close-knit group. The five of them had grown close since Shannon arrived in Apple Grove, and their support in times of need was priceless. "Whatever you want. I'll take you home to change, and then we'll head to town."

"Thank you." Kate settled back on the seat.

*　*　*

Twenty minutes later, Shannon maneuvered Old Blue into a parking space in front of the craft market. She'd barely stopped the truck before Kate opened the passenger door and jumped out.

Shannon joined her on the sidewalk and asked, "Do you

want me to tell the Purls about Millicent, or do you want to do it?"

Kate scrunched up her face. "Do we have to tell them at all?"

"I suppose not," Shannon said, taken aback by the notion. "But you know it will be all over town in a few hours anyway. It might be better if they hear the real story from us."

Kate's shoulders slumped. "In that case, would you mind telling them?"

"Not at all." Shannon patted Kate's arm and then opened the door to the store.

Cheerful voices drifted from Espresso Yourself, where Shannon had hastily left the Purls over an hour ago with little explanation. Melanie and Joyce still sat in the bright red leather chairs, and an avalanche of colorful sweaters covered them. Betty stood behind them, stacking and boxing sweaters with dangling white price tags.

"Well, I see you found Kate," Betty said, smiling.

Joyce lifted her head, took in Shannon and Kate's be-draggled look, and cringed. "And that's why I don't have a dog. Tough night walking Scarlet?"

"Not exactly," Shannon said, taking a seat. "There's something we need to tell you." She broke the news about Millicent's death and Eloise White's announcement.

"Now Grayson suspects me of killing Millicent," Kate finished, standing rigidly next to Shannon's chair.

"Oh, you poor thing!" Joyce assessed Kate with a ma-ternal look.

"Do you want something to drink?" Betty crossed over to Kate and gave her a quick hug.

Kate shook her head, and Betty gently led her to a chair. "Shannon, please tell us you're going to work on solving Millicent's murder so Kate's name isn't dragged through the mud." Joyce clutched her hand to her chest. "We'll all help you."

The other women murmured in agreement.

"I am, and I thank you for your offer to help. I will likely take you up on it in the near future." Shannon grabbed a sweater and price tag and then used a crochet hook to weave the string through the soft yarn. "As luck would have it, I'm fairly certain I saw the killer lurking outside of Millicent's house when I arrived."

Joyce leaned forward, her eyes wide. "What did he look like?"

"I can't say. He—or she—was nothing but a murky shadow."

Melanie tossed a blue-and-green striped sweater to Betty. "Millicent's murder isn't going to be easy to solve. Not with all of the enemies she made around town. The potential list of suspects will be pretty long."

Shannon tied a knot in the string. "You mentioned earlier that she moved here after her husband died. Does anyone know when that was?"

"Five years?" Betty glanced at Joyce. "Is that right?"

"Sounds about right," Joyce answered without looking up from the sweater she worked on.

"Does she have any family?" Shannon asked.

Joyce shook her head, sending her long, silver earrings swinging. "I'd heard that she was an orphan and had no family to take her in. She was raised in foster care; that's why she's protective of her money now. She had nothing for a good part of her life."

"'Protective' is a nice way of putting it," Melanie muttered.

A murmur of agreement traveled around the group. With such a general dislike of Millicent, Shannon's suspect list would indeed be quite lengthy.

"What about friends?" Shannon asked, hoping she could eliminate at least a few Apple Grove residents from her list.

Kate twisted the hem of her shirt between her fingers. "She doesn't have any friends that I know of. She keeps ... kept to herself."

"Now that you mention it, I've never seen her at any social events or with anyone from town," Betty added.

Shannon grabbed another sweater. "Then what about fellow dog owners?"

"Not likely. She's pulled many underhanded tricks on other owners in her quest to win," Kate said. "Some of those owners are currently in town for our show."

Betty's head popped up, her curly, auburn hair bouncing. "Do you think one of them would go so far as to kill her for revenge?"

Kate shrugged. "People have certainly killed for less."

"Is there money involved in winning a dog show?" Shannon asked.

"Not much." Kate paused, her expression growing pensive. "Showing a dog costs owners far more than the owner ever receives in prize money. But a major win can lead to big money in breeding the dog. Millicent wasn't planning to breed Scarlet, though."

Shannon felt the first good lead staring her in the face. "So what we're looking at is most likely a crime of passion."

"How do you figure?" Joyce asked.

"If I were the disgruntled owner of a rival show dog, and I arrived at Millicent's house *planning* to kill her, I wouldn't simply conk her over the head with a trophy. It might only wound her. No, I'd bring something with me to use as a weapon that I was certain would end her life. Like a knife, or a gun—or an untraceable poison."

Joyce nodded. "Remind me never to get on your bad side."

"Based on your description, it really does seem like the murder happened on the spur of the moment," Melanie agreed. "And since Scarlet is missing, it's only logical that one of the dog owners may be involved."

"I've been thinking the same thing," Kate said. "I truly think finding Scarlet will be the key to identifying the killer."

"You don't think she simply ran away?" Betty asked.

Kate shook her head. "With her training and a dog's natural instinct to remain with its injured owner, I really doubt it. Either way, I'd like to look for her. I plan to make a flyer to pass out at the show and post around town."

"We can help you with that." Melanie's face brightened as she looked at Kate. "As the chairperson for the show, you'll have your hands full this weekend. Our time is already committed to working the events, but maybe we can reorganize the schedule so we can search for Scarlet too."

"That's a great idea," Joyce said excitedly. "I say we start by taking Shannon off the schedule at our booth so she has more time to get to the bottom of this mess."

"Agreed," Betty added.

"Thank you," Shannon said. "As much as I'd love to see people buy our cute creations firsthand, with my other duties at the Espresso Yourself booth, I'll need every free moment available to untangle this mystery."

"What else can we do to help?" Melanie asked.

Shannon thought for a moment. "Betty, can you get me a list of the owners who've already checked in at the inn?"

"Sure."

"And I can give you the ones who are parking their RVs in the lot tonight," Kate offered.

"Brilliant," Shannon said. "Knowing which owners were in town tonight will give me a place to start in the morning."

"There's one thing I don't get," Melanie said. "If Millicent was supposed to be gone for the weekend, why was she home?"

"I have a theory on that," Shannon said. "While I was waiting for Grayson, I noticed that Millicent's car door was slightly open, so I took a quick peek inside. I found her keys in the ignition and her belongings in the car. I think she left home, realized she forgot something, and came back. When she went inside to retrieve it, the killer was already there. She surprised him, and he clocked her with the trophy."

Kate shuddered, and her gaze shot from person to person before finally landing on Shannon. "If I hadn't been running late for Scarlet's walk, *I* might have been his victim instead of Millicent."

An uneasy silence settled over the group. Shannon realized that if not for the luck of the draw, they might all be mourning the loss of their dear friend at that moment.

— 4 —

"I'm ready to call it a night," Shannon said to Kate as she put away the last of the clean dishes behind the coffee bar.

Kate continued scrubbing the countertop with fervor. The other Purls had already finished their jobs and headed home for the night, but Kate had insisted on helping Shannon clean up the coffee shop. Shannon would've been happy to leave the mess for morning, but she suspected Kate was using cleaning as an excuse to avoid going home—and she completely understood. She wouldn't want to be alone with the gruesome thoughts about Millicent's murder either. But after a very long day filled with physical labor, Shannon was worn out.

She took the towel from Kate. "I think it's time for both of us to head home to bed."

Kate frowned. "Maybe we should check to see if we missed pricing any of the sweaters."

"I've already checked; everything's ready. I have an idea. Why don't you come home with me and spend the night?" Shannon offered. "We can make some popcorn and watch a movie."

"I'm probably not going to sleep much tonight, and I don't want to keep you up."

"I don't mind."

"Thanks, but I don't want to put you out."

"Are you sure?" Shannon retrieved her coat from a stool.

"You won't be putting me out at all. I'd love the company. It gets lonely, rambling about in that big old mansion."

"I'm positive." Kate sounded resolved, but Shannon could see her friend's lingering anguish.

Shannon took Kate's hand. "Everything will be fine, sweetie."

"I hope so. I think it's going to take some time for me to get over finding Millicent ... that way." Kate freed her hand and grabbed her backpack from the counter.

"If you ever need someone to talk to about it, I'm always here for you." Shannon snapped off the coffee shop's lights. They stepped out into the night air, and she sifted her keys through her fingers until she settled on the one for the front door. She locked it and turned to Kate. "Shall I drop you at your apartment?"

"If it's not too much trouble."

"No trouble at all."

Lost in their own thoughts, they were both quiet during the short ride to Kate's. When Shannon pulled up in front of the building, she broke the silence. "Promise you'll call me if you need anything?"

Kate smiled. "I promise. And thank you for everything you did for me tonight."

"No need to thank me. That's what friends are for."

Kate climbed out of the truck, and Shannon backed onto the street and pointed her truck homeward.

She rolled the window down and inhaled the woodsy scent of smoke from a burning fireplace as she made the short trip home. As she turned onto the long drive of the Paisley mansion, the 1930s Mediterranean-style home she'd inherited from her grandmother, she noted how the full moon illuminated the round turrets and terra-cotta tiled roof, making it look like something out of a fairy tale.

She was surprised to see lights spilling through the front windows and over the lush grounds. Her housekeeper, Deborah Waters, usually retired at nine on the nose and left only one light on for Shannon if she wasn't home by then.

Something's wrong. Worried for the older woman, Shannon stopped in the circle drive and hopped out of her truck. She hurried up the stone stairs, the clipping of her heels echoing through the quiet. She entered the security code at the entrance, pushed open the door, and came to a stop when she heard Deborah's muffled voice.

Who could be visiting this late at night?

Shannon spun and checked to make sure she hadn't missed a visitor's car in the drive. No car.

A boisterous laugh rang out from the kitchen. Not just any laugh, but a distinct, loud cackle that Shannon would have known anywhere. She'd missed it something fierce. She rushed down the hallway toward the sound.

"Coleen?" Shannon burst through the kitchen door to find her dear friend seated at the island, a cup of tea in her hands. "Och, it *is* you!"

Shannon ran to Coleen and excitedly danced with her friend in the middle of the kitchen before throwing her arms around her. Standing a full head taller than Shannon, Coleen settled her arms over Shannon's shoulders and enveloped her in a bear hug.

After a long moment, Shannon pulled back. "When did you get here? What are you *doing* here? Is everything all right?"

"Quite frankly, no. I found myself missing you. Scotland isn't the same without you there. Are you surprised I came?" Coleen's lips broke into a wide grin.

"Very." Shannon held Coleen's hands "You should've told me you were coming. I would have picked you up at the airport. How'd you get here anyway?"

"I hired a cab."

Shannon clutched her chest. "From Scotland or from Portland?" she asked, laughing. "Either way, it must have cost a fortune."

"The look on your face was worth every penny, now wasn't it?" Coleen's big brown eyes were filled with mirth.

"You have no idea how happy I am to see you. Your timing is perfect. I could really use your advice—on a few things."

Deborah yawned and climbed off her stool. "I'll leave you two to catch up. I'm too old for late nights, and I can't stay up a minute longer."

Coleen returned to her chair with a spring in her step. "Phooey. You're as young as you feel."

Deborah laughed. "Then I must be as old as Methuselah. I'll see you both for breakfast."

"Good night," Coleen said. "And thanks for waiting up with me until this night owl got home."

"Night owl? It's only ten-thirty." Shannon grabbed a cup and filled it with tea from the blue delft teapot she'd received from her father many years ago.

Coleen held out her cup for a refill. "The Shannon I knew didn't stay out this late."

"Yes, well … the Shannon you knew had kids at home

and tried to keep them on a schedule. Now you're looking at a woman who is free as a bird."

Coleen stirred a generous portion of cream into her cup. "Minus the hours you spend working at the store and worrying over the twins while they're away at university. So what's that leave? Fifteen minutes of free time each day?"

Shannon grinned. "Ten."

"How are the twins adjusting to their new school?"

"I've not heard much from them since they started last month." Shannon took the stool next to Coleen. "But from what I have heard, they love it."

"Still struggling with the empty nest?"

"Not as much." Shannon took a sip of the warm Darjeeling tea. "Oh, I do miss them, but I've started to build an active life here, and I don't feel so alone."

A twinkle of mischief lit Coleen's eyes. "Speaking of alone, how is that deliciously single Michael Stone doing?"

"Surely you did not come all the way from Scotland to grill me about Michael," Shannon said gruffly, feeling a blush creep across her cheeks.

"I did, among other things." Coleen set her cup in the saucer and studied Shannon. "And from the look on your face, there's something you're not telling me."

Shannon sipped her tea.

Coleen bent low and leaned in close. "Shannon McClain, what are you hiding?"

"He asked me to go out with him this Saturday night."

Coleen's mouth dropped open. "On a *date*?" She squealed with joy and jumped from her stool. "Why didn't you call me? Oh, this is so exciting! We have so much to do to get you—"

Shannon held up her hand. "Before you get carried away, I don't know that it's a date. Technically, it's a 'thing' for his work."

"A 'thing'? That sounds mysterious—especially in his line of work." Shannon watched with amusement as her friend began to pace. "Perhaps he's taking you on a mob stakeout. With danger comes romance, you know. Or maybe he's planning to take you to the shooting range, where he'll be forced to envelope your slender frame in his strong arms as he shows you the correct way to hold the—"

"Stop, please." Shannon shook her head, unable to hold in her laughter. "You have got to start reading something besides romance novels. They're turning your mind to mush."

Coleen reclaimed her stool. "So define 'work thing.'"

"Michael said it's an annual banquet for his employees."

"Tell me more."

Shannon sighed. "I was so flustered by his invitation; I didn't think to *ask* much more. I know the event starts at seven. That's about it."

"Well, that's enough for us to plan your knock-him-dead outfit." Coleen furrowed her brows and grabbed a lock of Shannon's long red curls. "Now, what to do about your hair ..."

Shannon swatted her hand away and started to respond, but then she heard rustling outside the window. She spun around just in time to see a dark shadow cross behind the blind, then disappear.

She sucked in a surprised breath. "Did you see that?"

"Yes," Coleen said, clutching Shannon's arm. "It reminds me of the night when the man broke in here during my last visit. My goodness, are people still doing that?"

Shannon recalled that night, when she'd been attacked and had to fend off the intruder with a knitting needle. She exhaled and focused her thoughts. "Unfortunately, yes. Come on, let's go have a look."

Coleen clung to Shannon's arm as they crossed to the window. Shannon scissored open the blinds with two fingers so they could peek out. Coleen hovered close, and Shannon could hear her friend's quick breaths as their eyes searched the lawn.

"There," Coleen jabbed a finger through the blinds. "Someone's running away."

Shannon squinted and caught a fleeting glimpse of a figure darting down the expansive lawn and into the bushes.

Coleen's eyes widened. "Who do you think it was?"

"Perhaps it was nothing."

"*Nothing?*" Coleen frowned. "Have you gone daft?"

Shannon didn't answer.

Coleen met her gaze. "Something's going on that you haven't told me about. What are you keeping from me?"

Shannon let out a long sigh. "I'm not keeping anything from you. We just haven't had a chance to talk about it yet. I hate to burden you with this on your first night in town, but you're right, there is trouble afoot." Shannon told Coleen about Millicent.

"And you think the person lurking about your yard may have something to do with Millicent's death?" Coleen's voice waivered.

"It could be the same person I saw running away when I arrived at Millicent's."

"But why would he be here?"

Shannon pursed her lips. "I'm not convinced it was a man."

"Fine. To make it easy, let's just agree to say 'he.' Why was he here?"

"That I don't know." Shannon turned away from the window. "Maybe he thought I saw him clearly and can identify him."

Coleen grabbed Shannon's arm in a death grip. "Then that would mean he followed you home intending to ... to do something evil."

"Technically, he'd have had to follow me to the craft market first, then home," Shannon said, as the unsettling thought sunk in. If the person they'd just seen was indeed the killer, that meant he knew where she lived and worked. *Does he intend to kill me too?*

5

Yawning, Shannon padded toward the study. Her slipper-clad feet whispered across floors that gleamed in the morning sun shining through the window. She'd hoped to do a little research on the Internet and print out the photos of Millicent's house taken on her phone the previous evening, but she and Coleen had stayed up into the wee hours of the night, talking.

After their unwelcome visitor fled, Coleen had insisted on calling Grayson. Shannon had relented, though she knew he wouldn't be able to do much. After all the commotion died down, neither of them could sleep, so they chatted away most of the remaining night.

Tired or not, Shannon wanted Kate to review the pictures of Millicent's house today, even if it meant getting up early to print them.

She set her mug on the desk and connected her cellphone. After uploading the photos, she sent them to the printer. While waiting for the photos to print, she sipped the rich coffee blend she'd come to love almost as much as tea—a hazard of moving to a state filled with coffee connoisseurs. She opened her email, found an updated staffing schedule for the Purls' booth from Joyce, and added it to the print queue.

As the printer whirred and spit out pages, she enlarged a photo on the computer screen and studied it for any clue that might help her in the case. She noticed that in the middle of framed ribbons and certificates on the wall in Millicent's den, there was a faded square with an empty nail head.

Someone had removed a frame.

Curious, she continued looking through the pictures, stopping when she saw a circle surrounded by a thin layer of dust on a bookshelf indicating someone had removed an item. She grabbed her notepad and jotted a reminder to ask Kate about both items.

Her phone vibrated on the desk, and she glanced at the screen.

"Good morning, Beth," she answered.

"I hope I'm not calling too early." Her mother's voice sounded as warm as a downy quilt through the phone.

"Not at all," Shannon replied. "I'm up early for the dog show."

"I suspected you might have trouble sleeping after what happened to Millicent Downing last night."

Shannon felt her jaw drop. Though her mother had grown up in Apple Grove, Beth hadn't lived in town since her childhood, and she had only a few remaining connections with the townsfolk.

"How did you hear about that so quickly?" Shannon asked.

"If you remember, I'm staffing the shelter's booth today. I got here early in case anyone needed help, and a few of the locals are talking about the murder."

Of course they are. "You do realize Kate didn't kill Millicent, don't you?"

"That goes without saying," Beth said, then fell strangely silent.

"What are you not saying?"

"I'm worried that you'll try to hunt down the real killer and find yourself in danger, Shannon. I know how protective you are of your friends."

"I'll be careful. Will I see you later?"

"I'll be at the shelter's booth until one," Beth said. "Then I have to work." She owned Gourmet on the Go, a mobile gourmet food business with multiple food carts serving the greater Portland area.

"It's going to be a busy morning for me, but I'll try to stop by and say hello."

"I hope you can. Talk to you soon."

After they hung up, Shannon set her phone on the desk and glanced at the clock. Only ten more minutes to look at the pictures before she had to leave for the park.

"Who killed you, Millicent, and why?" she whispered as she stared at the screen, her mind filled with far more questions than answers.

As far as she could tell, the pictures of Millicent's house and car held no additional clues. She thought perhaps some clue in the photos might jump out at her if she had more information about Millicent's family.

She entered "Millicent Downing family" into an online search engine. The first listing included her late husband Robert's obituary. Shannon confirmed he'd been married to Millicent for thirty years, and he'd died five years earlier. No children or any members on Robert's side of the family were mentioned. If the obituary was correct, Millicent was Robert's sole surviving family member and beneficiary.

Shannon heard footsteps coming down the hall and

swiveled toward the door. Wearing a fluffy blue robe, Coleen entered the room. She ran her fingers through her tousled shoulder-length hair and stifled a yawn.

"I can't believe you're up this early after your long day yesterday," Shannon said.

"I could say the same thing for you." Coleen dropped onto a cushioned chair and rubbed her eyes.

"I needed to get an early start on my detective work—if you want to call it that." Shannon took a long, luxurious sip of coffee.

Coleen eyed her with suspicion. "They've turned you into a coffee drinker, I see."

"It's wonderful first thing in the morning when it's freshly ground like this." Shannon held up her mug. "Would you like to try a cup?"

"Och, no. I'll get some tea in a moment." She tipped her head at the computer monitor. "Do you have any leads on a suspect?"

"Not yet."

"Well then, let's talk about it. Maybe we'll come up with something—like Sherlock Holmes and his dear Dr. Watson. I'll be Watson. You can be the temperamental and insufferable Holmes." Coleen grinned.

Shannon chuckled. "You wouldn't mind?"

Coleen settled deeper into the chair. "I'd love the challenge. Where do we start?"

"Michael once told me the best first steps in an investigation are to look for means, motive, and opportunity. So I've been thinking about the other dog owners, but I'm not sure any of them have a strong enough motive to kill Millicent."

"Money is always a good motive for murder." Coleen steepled her fingers and rested her chin on the tips. "At least I see that on television shows. Do the winners of these dog shows make money?"

Shannon shook her head. "Not according to Kate."

"Hmm. You mentioned last night that Millicent was a wealthy widow. Maybe it's a family thing, and some destitute relative wants her money?"

"I've been researching that angle this morning, but it doesn't look like she *has* any family."

Coleen's eyes widened. "No family at all? How sad."

Shannon nodded her agreement. "If the gossip can be believed, she doesn't have any friends either. It seems as if no one but her dog is going to miss her—and her dog is missing too."

"How does someone go through life so alone, I wonder?" Coleen mused aloud.

"Based on what I heard last night from the Purls and the way she treated Kate, Millicent was cranky and demanding most of the time. She didn't go out of her way to make friends."

"Sometimes that's a cover-up for loneliness and not knowing how to reach out to others."

Shannon's heart filled with sadness and guilt. "If that's true, I hate to think that I could've done something to make her life better and didn't. But being so new in town, our paths hadn't crossed much yet."

Coleen patted Shannon's knee. "It's just like you to want to help, but you can't save everyone."

The alarm on Shannon's cellphone chimed, and she

ran a finger across the screen to silence it. "I set myself a reminder so I wouldn't get bogged down in research this morning and be late for my shift at the dog show."

"If you can wait for me to get dressed, I'll go to the show with you. I can't wait to see *everyone*." Coleen stood and winked at Shannon.

Shannon groaned., "And by 'everyone,' you mean Michael?"

An impish grin spread across Coleen's face. "For your information, I'm eager to see the Purls too. And of course, you know all about me and dog shows."

"What? You mean the fact that you've never been to one or ever heard of one before last night?"

"Touché, Holmes." Coleen's laughter bubbled out. "Touché."

"I need to get to the park to prepare my table, but if you can be ready in five minutes, I'd love for you to come along."

Coleen gaped at Shannon in horror. "Five minutes? Look at me. It'll take that long just to apply enough cover-up under my eyes to hide the dark circles."

Shannon laughed and slipped her arm around Coleen's shoulders. "In that case, Deborah's been up for hours, waiting to make breakfast for you. You can chat with her for a bit or even take a nap until I can come back and pick you up." Shannon steered them down the long hallway.

In the kitchen, Coleen sniffed appreciatively. "You are a woman after my own heart, Deborah."

Deborah's face crinkled with happiness. "Have a seat, and I'll bring you a plate and a cup of tea."

"That sounds brilliant." Coleen crossed the large kitchen to the adjoining breakfast area.

Shannon rinsed her cup and put it in the dishwasher before joining Coleen. "I'm meeting the Purls for lunch. I'll pick you up first, and then we can have lunch with the whole group. They'll be thrilled to see you again."

Deborah set a plate in front of Coleen filled with fluffy eggs, crisp bacon, and wheat toast. "I'm planning to go to the dog show this afternoon. I'd be happy to save you the trip and give Coleen a ride."

"That would be great," Shannon said, giving Coleen a quick hug. "I'm so glad you're here. I'm sorry I have to rush off and leave you."

A devilish expression spread across Coleen's face. "Let's hope you feel the same way after I've been in town for a while."

Laughing, Shannon traded her slippers for comfortable shoes and took the time to enjoy the crisp morning as she strolled to her truck. She rolled down her window for the drive and enjoyed the salty breeze whispering over her skin.

Once at the park, she made quick work of setting up her table. With no customers in line, she prepared Kate's favorite coffee, a double caramel latte, and then headed for the Ultimutt Grooming booth. As she walked along the shaded path, she couldn't shake the feeling that someone was watching her. She tried to brush it off, but the nagging feeling persisted.

Unease settled in, and Shannon slowed her pace. She quickly spun and surveyed her surroundings. A flash of movement down the path caught her attention, and her breath stilled. *Is someone really watching me, or am I just paranoid?*

People were milling around, and any one of them could have moved quickly. After a minute, she decided her overactive imagination was getting the best of her. It was broad daylight, and no one would try and harm her in front of so many witnesses. She brushed aside her concern and continued down the path. She spotted Kate organizing dog toys and grooming items at her booth. Kate had covered the inexpensive plastic tablecloth they'd put on last night with a bright fuchsia cloth boasting dog silhouettes along the hem.

As Shannon neared the table, Kate lifted her head and waved. With her long hair pulled back in a ponytail, Shannon could easily see the dark circles hanging like half moons under Kate's usually luminous eyes. She wore jeans and a T-shirt that read, "Rescued is my favorite breed." She was probably not making fans with the show owners, as they were all about the purity of their breeds, but Kate cared about saving the shelter and all lost and mistreated dogs—not making fans.

"I made your favorite." Shannon held out the coffee. At her friend's contented sigh of thanks, Shannon wondered if Kate had gotten any sleep at all.

Kate took a sip and then groaned with happiness. "Thank you. You don't know how much I needed this. It's been a rough morning."

Shannon's warning radar chimed. "Did something else happen?"

"Chief Grayson woke me up early with a search warrant."

"Looking for Scarlet?"

"Yes. He performed a thorough search of my apartment." Kate nodded at a metal folding chair for Shannon to take and then dropped into her nylon camp chair. "It didn't take long. Of course he didn't find her. Then the forensic expert accompanying him took a bunch of samples."

"Do you know what kind of samples?" Shannon asked.

"Dog hair." A pensive look crossed Kate's face. "Scarlet's never been to my house, but her hair could be there. I saw the tech looking in my hamper, and I haven't done laundry since her last grooming."

"Then you'll have a logical explanation for the hair being on your shirt."

"I also have a logical explanation for everything else Grayson has brought up, but that might not stop him from using the information to try and prove a case against me—and then arrest me."

"Try not to worry so much." Shannon smiled as she patted Kate's hand. "You've got the truth on your side and the power of the Purls behind you. We'll do everything we can to make sure that doesn't happen."

"I know you will. Thank you." Kate tapped a tall stack of bright orange papers on the table. "I've tried to take my mind off everything by keeping busy. I stayed up late to make flyers to pass out, and I've given some to the volunteers manning the show tent to hand out to every owner and visitor."

"What about the Purls' offer to help?" Shannon asked, worried that Kate was taking on too much when she was already under so much stress.

Kate pointed at the Purls' booth on the other side of the park, where Joyce, Betty, and Melanie filled the table with sweaters. "I've already given a stack to the girls. Once the local businesses open, they'll post the flyers."

"We should hand out flyers to all the vendors here too."

"I'm planning to—once they all arrive."

Shannon studied her friend with admiration. "You're a dynamo this morning. All that and you're table is ready for business."

"Yeah, I'm in good shape. How about you?"

"Everything's ready, but I need to keep an eye out for sleepy owners wandering out of their motor homes and trailers in need of caffeine." Shannon surveyed all the activity in the park. "If we don't make enough money to keep the shelter going, it won't be for a lack of trying."

Kate's lips turned up in a halfhearted smile. "I wasn't sure we could pull off something this big."

"We certainly couldn't have done it without *you* pushing us to work hard for your favorite cause."

"I wasn't too hard on you, was I?"

Shannon chuckled. "Not at all. I'm only teasing you."

"Oh. Sorry. I'm not in a very good mood this morning." Kate swirled her cup and stared into the coffee. "I don't suppose you have anything new to report about Millicent."

"No, but I did print out the pictures I took of her house and car. Now that you're over the initial shock, I was hoping you'd look at them to see if you notice anything amiss."

Kate sighed. "If you don't mind, I'd rather not do it right now. I'm in a bad enough mood from Grayson's visit, and I want to be cheerful for the morning customers."

Shannon studied her friend closely. It wasn't like Kate to put things off. "I realize you're upset about Millicent, but is there something else bothering you?" Shannon asked.

Kate's eyes filled with tears, and she sniffed as she looked up.

Shannon scooted closer to her friend. "You're scaring me, Kate. What is it?"

"I can't quit thinking about how Millicent looked. And about Scarlet wandering around town, frightened beyond words. Or that a killer might have taken her. She's such a precious little thing, and I'd hate for anything bad to happen to her. I mean, if someone could murder another human being, why would they even think twice about hurting a dog?"

Shannon took Kate's hand again. "Hey, don't worry about Scarlet. Grayson put out an alert on her last night. With all the Purls helping to get the word out this morning, we'll find her in no time."

"That's assuming she's just lost," Kate said. "Which I don't really believe."

"OK, then keep in mind Scarlet is worth a lot of money. It would be foolish not to keep her alive and well."

Kate blinked back her tears then nodded. "You're right. Hurting Scarlet would be like a jewel thief throwing away a diamond, wouldn't it?"

"Precisely." Shannon let go of Kate's hand and checked her booth for customers. "I probably should get going. I have to stop by the Purls' table to pick up the list of owners who arrived last night."

Kate gave a tremulous smile. "Let's hope it gives you a solid lead that will take us straight to the killer."

"Yes. Let's hope," Shannon agreed, but she knew from previous experience that finding a killer was never that easy.

— 6 —

A long line of sleepy dog owners stumbled down the sidewalk and followed the tantalizing aroma of freshly brewed coffee to Shannon's table. She'd been serving a never-ending line for two hours and wished she could take a break. She wiped the back of her hand across her forehead and quickly stretched her back.

Smiling at the next customer, she asked, "What can I make for you this morning?"

The thin woman at the front of the line held a prancing poodle on a jeweled leash and chatted with a short man who boasted a thick head of silvery hair.

"Two large mochas." The woman didn't bother to look at Shannon as she thrust her money across the table.

Shannon took the bills and started preparing the chocolaty coffee.

"Well who do *you* think did it?" Shannon heard the woman ask the man, so she stole another glance at the pair.

The man held up one of Kate's flyers. He looked at it, then shrugged. "If I had to put money on it, I'd say Gus Krause. He and Millicent fought all the time, and he's a cranky old dude."

Shannon nonchalantly moved to a spot that would allow her to make the mocha and eavesdrop better at the same time.

The man eased closer to the woman and lowered his voice. "Remember how Gus slipped that Pomeranian a dog chew laced with an antihistamine at nationals?"

A high, tinkling laugh slipped from the woman. "How could I forget? The Pom walked across the stage like a drunken sailor."

"Exactly!" the man exclaimed. "When Millicent figured it out and reported Gus, he was disqualified. He would've won the toy group that day if she hadn't."

Shannon made a mental note to ask Kate what a "toy group" was.

The woman spun, looking at the crowd. "Is Gus here today?"

"I haven't seen him yet this morning, but he was walking his Pom through the parking lot last night."

The woman covered her mouth with her hand. "Then that means he was in town when Millicent was killed."

Shannon snapped the lid on the first mocha and handed it to the woman, then finished the second one and gave it to the man. As soon as they walked away, she grabbed her notepad and scribbled, "Gus Krause, antihistamine, and toy group." She'd wondered how long it would take for the other dog owners to start gossiping about Millicent—apparently news among the set traveled fast.

She stowed her notepad and caught sight of the Paisley Craft Market manager, Essie Engleman, strolling down the sidewalk. Essie stood out from the crowd in her aqua T-shirt and the full skirt she'd sewn from silky scarves in bright colors.

"You look like you could use a break," Essie said as she slipped behind the table.

Shannon glanced at her watch. She would gladly give up barista duties so she could pursue her new lead, but Essie wasn't scheduled to staff the table until noon.

"You're not scheduled for another hour," Shannon said. "I don't want to infringe on your time off."

Essie waved a hand, her glittering fingernails catching the sun. "I could use the extra work."

"If you're sure ..."

"Go."

"OK. I'm off to do some sleuthing." Shannon slipped her apron over her head and handed it to Essie. "I have my cellphone on if you need to reach me."

Shannon grabbed her bag, which contained the list of dog owners provided by Betty and the pictures of Millicent's home and car. She slung it casually over her shoulder and picked her way through the growing crowd. A long line of customers stood in front of the Purls' dog sweater table and Kate's too, giving Shannon an idea. She slipped through the center of the park to join Betty and Joyce.

Shannon tugged Joyce to the side, causing her friend's many jeweled bracelets to jingle like a bell. "Have you heard anyone talking about Millicent this morning?"

Joyce's eyes widened. "No. Have you?"

"Only one couple, but I'm guessing similar conversations will pick up as word of her untimely demise spreads. Will you make it a point to pay attention to the gossip, and let me know what you hear?"

Joyce smiled enthusiastically, her full cheeks lifting. "No one's ever given me such a good reason to listen to gossip." She gave a mock salute. "You can count on me."

"Do you need a notepad to write on in case any names are mentioned as possible suspects?"

"Relax," Joyce said. "I've got this covered. I have the memory of an elephant."

Shannon chuckled. "Then it's a good thing you're not the type to hold a grudge. Can you pass the word on to Betty and Melanie too?"

"Aye aye, captain."

"When we meet for lunch, you can share anything you hear."

"Sounds like a plan," Joyce said before returning to the table.

Shannon disappeared into the crowd again. She slipped in and out of groups of people, their dogs yipping excitedly as she did. It wasn't the easiest place to be sneaky. Not only was the park overrun with the purebred dogs for the show, but many of the locals had brought their pets along for the day.

As Shannon approached Kate's table, she saw her friend's smile was quick and easy—like normal. Kate loved animals, and a park filled with dogs seemed to be the perfect salve to calm her anxiety.

"Excuse me a moment," Kate said to her customer before stepping away to join Shannon at the end of the table.

"Looks like you're as busy as I was this morning," Shannon said.

Kate nodded vigorously. "Not only are we raising a ton of money for the shelter, it's keeping my mind off … things."

Shannon cringed. "On that note, I hate to be the one to bring 'things' back to your mind." She pulled out the list of dog owners and pointed at Gus Krause's name. "But I heard a couple talking about Millicent's death while they waited for their coffee. They mentioned this man as a possible suspect in her murder. Do you know him?"

"Old Gus?" Kate's eyes widened. "He's a real curmudgeon, and he's ornery too. But I'd be shocked if he's her killer."

"What makes you say that?"

"His son was murdered in a home invasion—hence his perpetually bitter attitude. After going through that, I can't imagine he'd ever kill anyone."

Shannon felt her excitement slipping away. "I was hoping you'd say that he's the perfect suspect. Even so, I'll keep him on my list until I can officially rule him out. It's always possible he 'snapped' after his son's death and no longer lives by his previous moral code."

Kate chewed on her lip. "I suppose."

"Can I get a copy of today's schedule to see where I could find Gus?"

Kate retrieved the schedule from under her table. "The toy group is grooming now, so it would be a great time to talk with people who might have had an issue with Millicent."

Shannon took the list from Kate. "The couple I overheard talking mentioned the term 'toy group' too, and I wanted to ask you what that meant. Tiny dogs?"

"Well, basically. Dogs are broken into different groups for showing. The toy group is made up of the smallest breeds. Scarlet is in the toy class, and that means Millicent interacted with these owners on a regular basis."

"Brilliant." Shannon tucked the list in her tote bag. "Will you still be able to meet for lunch today, or are you too busy?"

"My cousin Tina is scheduled to relieve me. We're meeting at the craft market at noon, right?"

"Yes—and I have a surprise for everyone. A *good* surprise," Shannon added hastily.

"Then I'll be there. I could use a pleasant surprise." Kate smiled. "Oops, it looks like they need my help running the register. I'll see you at lunch." She hurried away to help a customer.

Shannon made her way down the busy sidewalk and slipped inside the grooming tent. Tiny dogs sat patiently on pedestals while their owners fussed with their hair. A blow dyer whirred at the far end of the space, and an occasional whine and whimper slipped from the little dogs. Shannon didn't recognize most of the dogs by their breed names, but her bag contained a reference chart with pictures. Kate had passed one out to each volunteer earlier to "increase their enjoyment in the volunteer experience." She quickly reviewed her chart and memorized a few of the breeds.

Attempting to fit in, Shannon moseyed into the space.

"Oh, what a gorgeous Maltese!" she exclaimed as she passed a pedestal, hoping she'd gotten the breed right. The owner puffed up with pride, and Shannon smiled in return. She continued on, listening to tidbits of conversations and commenting on the dogs as she went. "Ah, what an adorable Pekingese— I daresay he has an *excellent* chance of winning with a face like that." Shannon winked conspiringly at the owner.

The owner sniffed and looked down her nose at Shannon. "Winston is a *Shih Tzu.*"

"Right then. Carry on." Shannon gave a sheepish smile and quickly moved on.

She passed several pedestals before she finally heard Millicent's name mentioned. Squatting down, she pretended to tie her shoe so she could listen to the conversation unfold between a very skinny man and a woman wearing an absurdly large yellow hat. At the risk of sticking her foot in her mouth again, Shannon pulled out her chart and confirmed the man's miniature dog was a Chihuahua, and the woman's compact dog with hair flowing to the pedestal was indeed another Shih Tzu.

"I'll bet it was Lilly," the woman said, her dark curls bouncing with each syllable beneath the flying saucer on her head. "She couldn't be in the same room as Millicent without fighting with her."

The woman looked up from her Shih Tzu, her brush held in midstroke. "Millicent reported Lilly, didn't she?"

The man nodded.

The woman continued, "Not that I'm sticking up for Millicent, but Lilly deserved to be reported. I mean, she *dyed* her dog's coat. I can't ever keep Madame's coat white, so why should Lilly be able to use dye and get away with it?"

"I agree," the man replied. "Lilly deserved to be disqualified, but Millicent could've gone to her first and let her bow out gracefully. No need to embarrass her in front of everyone. That was just cruel."

"It gives Lilly a good reason to want to get back at Millicent—though I can't imagine resorting to murder over it."

"You never know what will set someone off. Way I see it, based on the way Millicent treated people, most everyone around here had a reason to be mad at her." The man picked up his pooch and cradled her close. "I need to check on my registration. Good luck in the competition."

As he departed, Shannon pulled out her notepad and wrote "Lilly dyeing her dog's coat." For the next hour, she made her way through the cramped space, interacting with the owners and listening for any mention of Millicent's name. As she did, the feeling that someone was watching her crawled over her again. She glanced behind her. No one seemed to be paying her undue attention. As she turned back, she thought she saw a large man dart behind a portable divider.

Am I truly paranoid, or is someone following me? She had to know.

She hurried across the tent, weaving in and out of the pedestals, until she reached the divider that segregated the first aid station from the rest of the space. Without slowing her pace, she rounded the corner and ran face first into the hard chest of a man built like a tank.

"Och!" she blurted.

The man made no move to steady her as she staggered backward. Instead, he folded his thickly muscled arms across his chest and scowled down on her.

"Can I help you with something?" His booming voice fit his size, and his gleaming bald head added to his menacing countenance.

"Funny," Shannon said, smoothing her hair while trying to regain some semblance of composure. "I was going to ask you the same thing."

"Do I know you?"

"Again, you've read my mind and stolen my question." She paused. "Why were you watching me?"

"Watching *you?*" he scoffed. "Lady, you're the one who just ran into me. All I'm doing is waiting for the nurse."

"Oh? Have you been bitten?" Shannon peered at what skin she could see on his crossed arms, looking for teeth marks. If by chance he was the murderer and had stolen Scarlet, maybe she bit him in the process. That would explain the blood found on the floor by Scarlet's crate.

"Here we are," the nurse said as she rounded the corner, carrying a box of large gauze bandages—the perfect size to cover a bite mark.

"If you'll excuse us," the man said to Shannon as he held out his hand for the box.

"Yes, of course," Shannon replied, but she continued to scan his arms as she backed out of the space. His skin appeared free from wounds, but that didn't clear him from suspicion. After all, Scarlet could have taken a small chunk out of his leg just as well as an arm.

If only Scarlet had been a German shepherd—a bite from a dog that size would be nearly impossible to hide!

7

Shannon set a large tray of sandwiches on the counter in Espresso Yourself and admired her handiwork. She'd artfully arranged sandwiches, cold drinks on ice, and large chocolate chip cookies among colorful napkins and plates to celebrate Coleen's return. She could hardly wait to see the Purls' surprised faces when they caught sight of her dear friend.

Bells above the door jangled, and Shannon turned to greet her friends. When she spotted Michael ushering Coleen through the door, Shannon felt her jaw drop open. *How had Coleen sniffed him out so quickly?*

His olive green shirt highlighted his black hair and made him look even more handsome than usual. He stood next to Coleen with perfect posture, a fond facial expression softening his intense gaze. Shannon felt the warmth of a blush rush up and over her face as their eyes met. The urge to look away was strong, but she kept her cool and smiled at him instead. He returned it with a dazzling smile of his own, drawing Coleen's attention. With a raised eyebrow, she slipped her hand in the crook of his arm and led him toward Shannon.

"Thanks for inviting me to lunch," he said to Shannon when they stopped near her.

Shannon blinked. "I didn't—"

"She didn't want you to go hungry," Coleen interjected smoothly.

Michael cast a skeptical glance at Coleen, then Shannon. He clearly hadn't missed Shannon's surprise at his arrival.

Not wanting him to feel awkward, Shannon gestured toward the bar. "I'm glad you could join us. Everything's ready if you want to fix your plate."

"If you have a minute, I'd like to talk to you before we eat."

A broad smile broke out on Coleen's face. "I'll give you two some privacy." She sauntered away, a satisfied grin on her face.

Shannon turned her attention to Michael. "What's on your mind?"

"Your safety." His expression turned serious. "You didn't tell me you saw someone fleeing the crime scene last night, or that you saw a person lurking outside your window."

"You've talked with Grayson, I see," Shannon said, wondering where the conversation was headed. Clearly, Michael was annoyed with her.

"I wish *you* would tell me these things. I suspect the person outside your window was the same person you saw running away from Millicent's house—a murderer."

"I had exactly the same thought." She paused, debating whether or not to tell him about her morning.

"I know that look," Michael said. "Spill it."

"It's probably nothing, but I had the distinct feeling someone was following me this morning." Shannon filled him in on her day.

Michael exhaled sharply. "The man at the nurse's station, did you get his name?"

"No, but he's very unique looking, so maybe someone at the dog show knows him." She described the man to Michael.

"I'll be on the lookout for him." He lifted a hand as if planning to touch her, then let it drop to his side. "Please be careful."

The urgency in his voice touched her. She looked away to still her emotions and spotted the Purls through the front window approaching the shop. The door opened, and they all shuffled in, looking worn out from the busy morning.

"Coleen!" Joyce cried out, her eyes growing large. "I didn't know you were visiting."

"Aye. Surprise!" Coleen's mouth tipped in a camera-worthy smile.

Joyce grabbed Coleen in a big hug, and they swung around in a circle together.

Melanie turned to Shannon. "I can't believe you were able to keep her visit a secret from us."

"It wasn't hard. She surprised me too."

"How fun!" Melanie clapped her hands.

A happy smile lit Kate's face, but she was still less than her usual enthusiastic self.

Coleen wrapped an arm around Kate's shoulders and squeezed. "My poor, sweet girl. Don't you worry. We'll work out this problem in no time."

Melanie stepped up to Coleen for a hug, and Betty stood waiting for her turn.

Shannon turned to Joyce. "I'm so glad you found someone to staff the table so all of you could come to lunch."

"How could my loving husband possibly say no to *moi*?" Joyce winked and grinned mischievously.

Everyone laughed, and Shannon gestured for her guests to help themselves to lunch. Michael insisted the women go first and stood back while they lined up.

Feeling his eyes on her, Shannon loaded her plate with food. She joined the Purls and Coleen in the plush chairs, balancing her plate on her lap. Looking a bit uncomfortable with a room full of women, Michael perched at the counter. For the next thirty minutes, they chatted about Coleen's trip. When the conversation wound down, a gentle quiet born of good friends settled around them.

Seeing plates nearly empty, Shannon got up and grabbed the cookies. She handed the plate to Joyce.

"Perfect." Joyce chose one and passed them on.

Melanie settled her empty plate on the table and took a cookie. "What do you have planned while you're in town, Coleen?"

"Not a thing other than spending time with you all," Coleen answered. "Now that Kate has found herself in the middle of an unfortunate canine calamity, I plan to spend a lot of time at Shannon's side, trying to help solve the mystery behind it."

"Speaking of that," Betty said, "Joyce and I overheard a customer say a woman named Cassandra recently had a very vocal fight with Millicent at a dog show. I gathered Millicent did something to make this Cassandra person really angry."

Joyce's eyes took on a devilish glint. "I tried to ask the guy more about it, but he clammed up on me. Guess I'm not the super sleuth you are." She winked at Shannon. "Yet."

"Ha! If you'd seen me trying to act like a dog expert

today, you wouldn't be so complimentary," Shannon replied. "Can either of you think of anything else that could be important?"

Betty thought for a moment. "After they stepped away, I did hear the man mention Doggie Delights, but they could have been talking about something else by then."

Kate sat forward. "Millicent was killed with the trophy Scarlet won in a show sponsored by Doggie Delights!"

"So this could be important then?" Betty asked.

"Yes." Shannon pointed to the clipboard on Kate's lap. "Kate, can you look up Cassandra's name on your registration list and tell me if she has a dog entered in the competition?"

"Sure." Kate pulled the clipboard out from under her plate. "I see a Cassandra Presley. She's showing a toy poodle."

Shannon whipped out her notepad and scribbled. "I've also heard comments about a woman named Lilly. Do you have a Lilly on your list?"

Kate ran her finger down the form. "There's a Lilly Lansdown with a Shih Tzu."

"Lilly's another suspect?" Michael asked.

Shannon nodded, choosing to ignore his dubious tone. "We don't know what happened between Millicent and Cassandra yet, but I heard that Millicent got Lilly disqualified for dyeing her dog's hair."

"That's a major offense in the show dog world," Kate said.

Michael picked up his soda can. "And you think that's cause for murder?"

Kate shook her head. "Shannon seems to, but I'm not as sure. Getting disqualified from one show isn't worth killing someone over, in my opinion."

"But you're not one of the diehard show people outside," Michael said, mocking a shudder. "From what I saw this morning, they're a pretty intense bunch."

"My thoughts exactly." Shannon smiled at him for weighing in on her side. "I agree it would take someone a bit unhinged to commit murder. But some people snap more easily than others."

"So what you're saying is," Coleen said, grinning, "to do something like this, the person would have to be ... 'barking' mad."

For a second, no one spoke. Then Joyce let out a snort and began to laugh, and everyone else joined in.

"Brilliant," Shannon said. "Have I told you how much I've missed you, Coleen?"

Even Kate chuckled and seemed to relax a bit amidst the silliness. She settled the clipboard on her lap. "I wish we'd hear something about Scarlet."

"The park is flooded with your flyers," Michael said. "If someone finds her running loose, they're bound to call you."

Kate focused on Betty. "Were you able to get the flyers posted in the businesses around town this morning too?"

Betty nodded. "Plus the manager at the grocery store said he'd put one in every customer's bag if we could bring some over there."

Kate's lips curved into a smile. "I'll run some off as soon as I finish eating."

The bells jingled above the entrance, and Kate's smile fell. Shannon turned and glanced over her shoulder. She watched as Chief Grayson stepped into the store and headed straight for the archway leading to the coffee shop.

"I hope I'm not interrupting anything," he said as he approached Kate, "but I have a few more questions for you, Kate. Do you have a minute?"

Kate set her plate on the table. "My appetite is gone, so I do now."

The chief looked around at the group. "Maybe we should step outside for privacy."

Kate clutched Shannon's arm like a lifeline, her fingers digging in deep. "I want Shannon with me. It's either that or I'm not talking to you without a lawyer present."

Shannon pried Kate's fingers free and held her friend's hand. "I really don't think Kate should be alone right now."

Grayson gave them both an irritated look and then turned a pointed gaze on Michael.

Michael smiled down on the group. "Ladies, why don't we finish our lunch outside to give them some privacy?"

"That would be lovely," Coleen said, smiling up at him.

Grayson fixed Shannon with a stern look. "Be advised, if you stay, anything we discuss is confidential."

"Of course," Shannon said.

The other ladies looked at her, and she smiled to let them know it was all right to leave. They got up and followed Michael outside.

"Would you like some lunch, Chief?" Shannon offered.

"No, but I wouldn't mind a cold drink and sitting down for a few minutes."

Shannon pointed at the bar. "Feel free to help yourself."

Grayson wedged his cap under his arm and stepped to the counter. His balding head glistened under the fluorescent lighting. He selected a cola, popped the top open, and returned to where they sat.

"Is there any word on Scarlet?" Kate asked.

"I'm afraid not." Grayson took a long sip of his soda and sat in the chair vacated by Melanie. "We still have an alert out on her. Plus, one of my men has been checking online for any sale ads for dogs matching Scarlet's description."

"What about Millicent's murder?" Shannon asked. "Has anything been determined about the cause?"

"The ME has confirmed the trophy is our murder weapon, and our crime techs have finished processing Millicent's house. They've lifted two sets of prints." Grayson paused and let his stare drill into Kate. "Millicent's and yours."

Kate crossed her arms. "If you're trying to shock me, it won't work. I've taken care of Scarlet for years now. I'm sure my prints are all over that house."

Grayson set his soda on the table. "And taking care of her includes getting your prints on her trophies?"

Kate shrugged. "No crime in looking at them as far as I know."

Grayson studied her for a long moment. "You mentioned last night that you and Millicent didn't always agree."

"Yeah. So?"

"You failed to mention that Millicent filed a lawsuit against you."

Lawsuit? Shannon stared incredulously at Kate.

Kate's face creased in horror. "It was nothing."

"Tell me about it anyway," Grayson demanded as he pulled a small notepad from his shirt pocket.

Kate drew in a deep breath as if fortifying herself.

"Scarlet found a pack of gum in Millicent's purse. She got the gum tangled in her coat, and Millicent brought her to me to groom. I told Millicent it would be painful for Scarlet if we tried to remove the gum by combing it out. I said that I could cut it out, and it wouldn't be very noticeable. She authorized me to proceed, and when she came back for Scarlet, she was horrified at what I'd done. She had a show the next day, and she said the judges would see it. She got mad at me and stormed out. A week later, I was served with papers over the incident."

Grayson sat forward. "Then what happened?"

"I went to talk with her and got her to drop the charges."

"What did it take?" Grayson asked, his pen poised over the notebook.

"I had to offer her free pet-sitting for a year."

Oh, you poor, sweet thing, Shannon thought.

Grayson's brow shot up. "Do you have any proof of that arrangement?"

"No, but the lawsuit was dropped. We'd obviously re-solved things, or she wouldn't have allowed me to continue to work with Scarlet."

Grayson settled back in his chair again. "Who else be-sides you knew Millicent would be away for the weekend?"

Kate shrugged. "I mentioned it to Shannon last night, but I don't remember telling anyone else."

Shannon cleared her throat. "Where are you going with all of this, Grayson?" she asked.

He ran a hand over his balding head, settling the few remaining strands of hair in place. "If Millicent's neighbors thought she'd left town, Kate could take Scarlet and kill

Millicent without fear that anyone would discover the body for a few days. It would take awhile for Millicent to be missed—plenty of time for Kate to try to cover her tracks."

"If that's true, then why did Kate call me right away?" Shannon held up her hand. "And before you say to secure my help in covering up the crime, why did I turn around and call you?"

Grayson scowled. "*Did* you turn around and call me, or did you wait until much later?"

Irritation flooded through Shannon at his audacity to insinuate her involvement. "The medics said Millicent's body was still warm, so you know the answer to that already. And you probably know the time of death too. Compare that with the time of my call, and it will prove I didn't wait."

"Speaking of that, let's talk about the time of Millicent's death." Grayson paused, his attention riveted on Kate. "Where were you between five and seven last night?"

"I was at church, picking up the folding chairs for the show."

"It took two hours to pick up chairs?"

Wariness crept into Kate's expression. "Each week, church volunteers are assigned cleaning duties. It was my weekend to clean. I knew I'd be tied up all weekend with the show, so I cleaned first."

"Was anyone else at the church with you?"

"No. The staff had already gone home for the day." Kate swung her gaze to Shannon. "You know I was there, right? I mean, I came back with the chairs."

"That you did," Shannon answered. "And then you were with me at the park the rest of the time."

Grayson's focused attention didn't waiver from Kate. "But for all Shannon knows, you could've swung by Millicent's house, hit her with a trophy, and then went to the church."

Shannon sighed. "With all due respect, you're talking in circles, Grayson."

"You're not going to arrest me, are you?" Kate sounded dazed.

"No." The chief stood and peered down at her. "At least not yet, but I can't ignore the facts for long."

"Tell him what you found out today, Shannon," Kate implored.

Shannon nodded. "Grayson, I understand that you have to look at Kate as a possible suspect, but I uncovered two more potential suspects this morning that you'll probably want to look into." She told him about Gus Krause and Lilly Lansdown's underhanded tricks, but she didn't mention Cassandra, as she didn't have enough details about their spat yet.

"Thanks for the heads-up." He jotted down their names. "As the event organizer, Kate, I assume you're the one to provide me with a schedule, so I can find Gus and Lilly."

Kate tapped her clipboard. "I only have the master schedule with me, but I'll make a copy for you."

"What about the people who might stand to inherit Millicent's money?" Shannon asked. "Are you looking into them?"

"Of course," Grayson said.

"Who might that be?"

"You let me worry about that."

Shannon felt her ire rise, but Grayson was known for

keeping things close to the vest, and it would do no good to get mad at him for not sharing.

Grayson pushed back his chair and stood. "That's all for now, Kate, but don't forget my reminder not to leave town, you hear?"

Kate nodded.

With one last look at Shannon, he pressed his hat on his head and departed.

Tears formed in Kate's eyes. "Can you clear my name before he arrests me, Shannon? You know I'm innocent."

Shannon searched for an answer that would make her friend feel better, but she couldn't come up with anything that wasn't a lie. After Grayson's bombshell about the lawsuit and Kate's lack of alibi on top of everything else, for the briefest of moments, the thought that Kate might have been somehow involved in Millicent's death didn't seem all that far-fetched.

8

Shannon gave herself a hard mental shake, feeling guilty for even entertaining the thought that Kate could have had anything to do with Millicent's death. *Kate would never harm a person, not directly or in partnership with someone else. Not even to help a dog ... surely not.*

"I can't believe Grayson found out about the lawsuit," Kate said as she flung herself back in her chair and crossed her arms. "I've never told anyone about that. I figured after Millicent dropped it that no one in town would find out about it. Now it's bound to come out. I hope I don't lose business because of it."

"Any lawsuit becomes public record once filed," Shannon said. "Grayson would naturally check all court documents involving Millicent to find out if anyone had a motive to kill her." She tipped her head in an understanding nod. "With Millicent's reputation, I'm sure your customers will understand."

Kate's expression brightened slightly. "I hope so."

"Do you remember the name of Millicent's lawyer?"

The hopeful gleam faded from Kate's eyes. "I have his business card at the shop. Why?"

"I searched the Internet to see if Millicent had any relatives. I didn't find any, but maybe this attorney knows of a family member or anyone else who might be after her money. I might even be able to find out whom she named in her will."

"Her will?" Kate's face turned strangely pale. "Do you really think her attorney would give out that kind of information? I'd hate for you to waste your time."

"He might not tell me anything, but you heard Grayson's response to my question. He won't tell me who stands to inherit, so I have to try and find another way to get the information."

Kate's eyes glistened with tears again. "As far as I know, Millicent was all alone. I'll bet she left everything to Scarlet."

The front door opened and Coleen poked her head inside. "Is it OK for us to come in now that Grayson has gone?"

"Yes," Shannon said, glad to have Coleen's help in getting Kate off her emotional rollercoaster.

Coleen pressed the door wide and she, along with the other Purls, entered the coffee shop. They all looked exhausted—save for Coleen. She charged into the room with her usual high-octane attitude. "Michael had to go back to work. He said he'd talk to you later, Shannon." She paused near Kate and fixed an appraising stare on the younger woman. "I take it from your expression that Grayson didn't bring good news."

"I'm still tops on his suspect list." Kate told them about the lawsuit and her lack of an alibi.

Betty rested a hand on Kate's shoulder. "Don't worry. Shannon will figure this out, won't you, Shannon?"

"Of course. For every mystery, there is an answer," she said, forcing a confident smile for Kate's sake.

"As much as I'd like to stay and chat, I need to go cover Carrie for her lunch break," Melanie said.

Coleen clapped her hands, startling everyone. "Before you go, I wondered ... have you all heard Shannon's exciting news?"

Shannon noticed Coleen deliberately avoiding her gaze, which generally meant her dear friend was up to something. "Coleen ..."

Coleen batted her lashes innocently and waved at Melanie to sit down. "Judging by your reactions, I take it you all don't know."

"What's this about?" Kate whispered to Shannon.

Shannon narrowed her eyes at Coleen. "One never knows with Coleen."

"And that's why we all love her so much," Betty laughed as she took a seat across from Shannon. "Never a dull moment."

"Come on already," Joyce encouraged. "We're dying to know what your big news is, Shannon."

Shannon furrowed her brows at Coleen. "I'm just as curious as you are."

Coleen grinned. "OK. I am thrilled to report ..." She paused, upping the ante of everyone's interest. "... that our very own Shannon McClain has a *date* on the books for this Saturday night! I knew you'd all be as happy for her as I was when I heard the news."

All heads whipped in Shannon's direction, mouths agape.

Melanie blinked. "A date?"

"Really?" Betty asked.

"With whom?" Joyce sputtered.

At Shannon's stunned expression, Coleen leaned in and answered, "Michael Stone. Saturday night."

Shannon felt her face flush under the intense scrutiny and blurted out the first thing that came to mind. "Before you all go nuts on me, it is *not* a date."

"Then what is it?" Kate asked.

"A work function." Shannon cleared her throat. "He asked me to accompany him to a dinner party they hold for their employees every year. It's nothing to get so excited about." She shot Coleen a pointed look.

"Work functions can count as dates," Betty offered. "Did he specifically say it *wasn't* a date?"

"Well no, but I—"

"I have it on good authority that it's more than a platonic work function," Coleen interrupted.

Shannon groaned, imagining Coleen badgering Michael about the dinner during the few minutes they'd had alone, asking him awkward and uncomfortable questions as only Coleen could. "Please tell me you didn't say anything to embarrass me—or him."

Coleen perched on the arm of Kate's chair and adopted an air of indignance. "Of course not. He's the one who brought it up, and from what he said, I know he's looking at this as more than 'just friends.'"

"I'm so happy for you! What are you going to wear?" Melanie asked.

Shannon's heart fluttered. "I haven't really given it much thought."

"We can help you." Kate sat forward, all traces of her angst gone. "Is the event formal or casual?"

"I don't know. I didn't ask. All he said was it's an employee appreciation dinner being held in a Portland hotel."

Coleen *tsked*. "I guess I'll have to talk to him about it again." She grinned at Shannon. "How *do* you manage to get by without me around?"

"I can't imagine," Shannon said flatly. "And don't you dare talk to him about it again. We're not teenagers. I'm perfectly capable of asking him myself."

"I know you are, love, but it's much more fun if I do it, now isn't it?" Coleen kept her eyes on Shannon, who was clearly growing more annoyed by the second.

"Coleen—"

Coleen giggled. "That got a rise out of you now, didn't it? Don't worry. I'm only kidding. I won't say a word."

"M-hm." Shannon stood. "I should get going and relieve Essie for lunch." She placed a hand on Coleen's shoulder. "Do you want to come with me or spend some time here, catching up with the girls?"

"Do you mind if I stay?"

"Not if you promise to stay out of trouble." Shannon squeezed her friend's shoulder. "Come find me when you're finished."

As Shannon stepped outside, she heard her mother call out to her and turned to see Beth waving from across the street. Shannon wound her way down the sidewalk and crossed the street to meet her. Each time Shannon saw Beth, she was struck by how her fiery red hair and deep green eyes matched that of her twin teenagers.

"I'm glad I found you," Beth said breathlessly. "The afternoon volunteer for the shelter booth still hasn't shown up. I need to get to work, but I don't want to leave the booth unstaffed."

"Let's talk to Kate," Shannon answered, but her gaze wandered to Grayson, who stood a short distance away, chatting with a woman Shannon didn't recognize. "She has the list of volunteers, and she should be able to find a replacement."

Beth stepped into Shannon's sightline to recapture her attention. "Would you mind talking to her about it while I go back to watch the booth?"

Shannon memorized the woman's features and reluctantly focused on her mother. "No problem."

"You seem distracted. Is everything OK?"

Shannon nodded, but it was a halfhearted attempt, and her mother's eyes narrowed in scrutiny.

"I'll go talk to Kate," Shannon said quickly to keep Beth from worrying. "Either Kate or I will stop by the booth shortly to let you know what's going on." Shannon turned and crossed the street to her shop.

Kate stepped outside, squinting in the bright sunshine. She held her clipboard and a copy of the schedule for Grayson.

Shannon told Kate about the volunteer not showing up. "I hoped you'd have someone else in mind."

Kate flipped the pages on her clipboard and ran her finger down a column of names. "Everyone's slotted in this afternoon. Do you think Beth would agree to stay?"

"I'm sure she would, if she didn't need to get to work," Shannon said. "I'd do it, but I have to relieve Essie."

Kate gestured ahead. "Isn't that your mother coming our way now?"

Shannon turned and caught sight of Beth's vivid red

hair as she quickly made her way through the crowd. "That's odd. She said she was going back to the table."

"We'd better find out what's going on." Kate set off, and Shannon followed her across the street.

"Don't worry about finding a replacement." Beth paused to draw in a deep breath. "The table's covered."

"By who?" Kate asked.

"A couple of the owners who've already shown their dogs stopped by the table and volunteered."

Kate fired a disapproving look at Beth. "But who are they, and are they qualified?"

Beth smiled apologetically. "I'm sorry, but I didn't check them out. As dog owners, I figured they could answer any questions easily enough. They seemed eager to help."

"Thank you for taking care of it," Shannon said, giving Kate a pointed look.

"Oh, right," Kate agreed belatedly. "I should be thankful for your help instead of jumping down your throat. I'm sorry. I have a lot on my plate right now."

"I understand," Beth said. "Does this mean I'm still on the schedule for tomorrow?"

"Yes, yes, of course," Kate said.

"Then I'll see you both tomorrow." After a warm look for Shannon, Beth hurried away.

"I made a mess of that, didn't I?" Kate sighed. "I hope I didn't offend her."

"She knows you're under a lot of stress."

"I'm going to go find out who the volunteer people are, give this schedule to Grayson, and make more copies of the flyers. I'll see you later." Kate departed with renewed purpose.

Shannon returned to the Espresso Yourself booth and was welcomed by a line ten people deep waiting to order. She slipped behind the table and donned a bright red apron.

Essie's head popped up from the drink she was blending. "Thank goodness! I could use the help to get this line taken care of."

"What about your lunch break?" Shannon smoothed the wrinkles out of her apron.

"I'll go once we get through the rush." Essie handed an iced drink to a woman with a small child in tow. "How about I take the orders and you fill them?"

"Sounds perfect." Shannon stepped to the far end of the table.

Essie called out the first drink, and Shannon dove into the work. She worked at a frenzied pace for the next thirty minutes, completely in a zone. But when she heard two women discussing Millicent, she stopped mixing drinks and watched as they approached her end of the table. One of the women, a tall, willowy brunette, wore a contestant's nametag that read "Grace Givens." Shannon didn't recognize her or her friend as being the woman she'd seen Grayson talking with earlier.

"And that's not all." The friend inched closer to Grace and lowered her voice slightly. "On the way up to my room last night, I actually heard someone say they thought *I* could've killed her! Can you believe it?"

"Oh, Lil, you can't be serious!" Grace exclaimed.

Lil? As in Lilly Lansdown? Shannon leaned over and craned her neck to try and read the registration badge pinned on the woman's tank top, nearly knocking over a cup of coffee in the process. *Yes! Hello, Lilly.*

"It's preposterous," Lilly declared, planting well-manicured fingers on her curvy hips. "To think I'd do such a thing. I wouldn't hurt a flea."

A wiry man in a bad toupee snorted from behind them. Lilly spun. "What's your problem, Gus?"

Gus Krause? Shannon glanced at his badge for confirmation.

"Way I hear tell," he said, "Millicent ratted you out for dyeing your dog's coat. Seems like reason enough to want to get back at her. I know firsthand how you can hold a grudge."

"Millicent got you disqualified too," Lilly snapped. "Perhaps you killed her?"

Gus rolled his eyes. "Course I didn't."

Lilly crossed her arms, her silvery polish flashing in the sunlight. "Well, neither did I. If you don't want to be sued for defamation of character, you'd best stop suggesting that I did."

"You tell him, Lil." Grace said, slipping her hand into the crook of Lilly's arm and pulling her friend's focus back toward the counter.

Lilly glared at Shannon. "What's taking so long with my iced coffee?"

Shannon jumped. "I'll have it up in just a second."

Keeping her ears open, Shannon picked up her pace. As soon as the line dropped to three people, Essie left for lunch, and a steady stream of customers kept Shannon busy. When Essie returned, she couldn't believe an hour had already passed.

"I hate to do this to you, but can you handle this alone again for awhile?" she asked Essie.

Essie pushed up her sleeves. "Piece of cake. I take it you have a good lead to pursue?"

"Let's hope."

Leaving Essie in charge, Shannon wound through the crowd that had doubled in size since lunchtime. She found Gus easily enough, standing by himself outside the main tent. He seemed preoccupied with watching other people and didn't notice her approach at first. Given the way he'd acted in line, she believed him to be a straightforward kind of guy, so she decided to skip the pleasantries.

"Gus, I heard you had a run-in with Millicent Downing," she said, playing up her Scottish accent and trying to inject a royal authority in her tone. "I'd like to speak with you about it."

If her statement surprised him, his blank expression didn't give him away. "I've already told the other cop all I know about her."

"I'm not a cop."

He eyed her with suspicion. "Who are you?"

"A concerned resident."

"Then I surely have no reason to talk to you," he said. "Take your concern elsewhere."

Undaunted, Shannon pulled out her notepad and pen. "Am I to assume you have something to hide then?"

"Course not. I didn't kill Millicent."

"She was the reason you were disqualified in a show though, right? She cost you a trophy." Shannon took a quick peek at her notes. "Something about an allergy medicine."

"No," he snapped. "*I* was the reason for my disqualification. *I* drugged a competitor's dog. Millicent merely reported it."

Shannon blinked with surprise. Gus taking responsibility for his outlandish actions wasn't quite the reaction she'd expected. "You weren't upset with her then?" she asked.

He shrugged. "Upset, yeah—but I wouldn't kill her over it. I'm not deranged or anything."

In her gut, Shannon actually believed him, but she knew gut feelings didn't prove anything. "Where were you between five and seven last night?"

"Like I told the cop, my wife and I were on our way here. We stopped for gas around six-thirty." He pulled out his wallet and withdrew a receipt. "Check the time stamp and location. I have a lead foot, but even so, we couldn't have gotten here in thirty minutes."

She examined the receipt and discovered he was telling the truth. Mentally crossing him off her suspect list, she asked, "Do you have any thoughts on who might want to kill Millicent?"

"I've heard Kate Ellis's name mentioned as a suspect. She's the lady who found the body—or so she claims."

"What have you heard, exactly?" Shannon asked, hating that people were gossiping about her friend.

"Kate threatened to take Scarlet away from Millicent. When Millicent got upset, Kate got angry and hit her. Kate's a real softy, so I could see her wanting to take Scarlet from a strict owner like Millicent."

Shannon hoped others weren't thinking the same thing. "Do you honestly believe she did it?"

"Either her or Peter Needlemeyer. Not only was he tossed out of a show for decking her, but he was banned from competing for one year because of it. The man has some serious anger management issues."

"Wait a second, you mean this Peter guy actually *hit* Millicent?"

"Yep." Gus shook his head. "Talk about a guy who should be locked up."

"You wouldn't happen to know where I can find him, would you?" she asked, excited—and disgusted—by the promising lead.

"See that tall guy with the bald head?" Gus pointed down the sidewalk.

Shannon searched the crowd until her gaze landed on an imposing man who stood a head taller than everyone else in the crowd. Her stomach filled with dread. *The man I ran into in the first aid area.* She would rather Gus had pointed to anyone besides the tower of a man whose perpetual scowl sent a chill down her spine.

"You don't mean the one who looks like Mr. Clean?" she asked, hopeful that he didn't.

"That's the one."

Shannon put a hand over her eyes to shade the sun and peered at Peter Needlemeyer again. Questioning a man who'd already proven his disregard for women with physical violence was going to take every ounce of courage Shannon possessed—and then some.

9

Gusty winds whipped against Shannon, veering her slightly off course as she approached Peter Needlemeyer. He stood rock solid like a massive Oregon pine and glowered down at her, his icy blue eyes piercing her with doubt as she stopped before him.

At her side, she clutched the large bottle of grooming spray that she'd swiped off a nearby table, her finger poised on the trigger. Not the ideal weapon, but if Mr. Needlemeyer got squirrelly, he'd be choking on citrus and baby powder for days.

"Hello again." Shannon looked the man square in the eye. "Could you spare a minute to talk with me about Millicent Downing?"

He folded his arms across his broad chest. A long leash leading to a fluffy white dog dangled over one muscled forearm. "You're like a bad penny."

Shannon swallowed hard and plunged ahead. "I'm looking into Millicent's murder for a friend of mine. I understand you and Millicent had an altercation last month."

Peter lifted his hand and Shannon instinctively stepped back, her finger accidentally pressing on the sprayer. When his massive paw landed on his shaved head, Shannon dared to breathe—then gagged as the heavily scented spray filled her lungs. "Och, goodness, that's strong."

Too late, she realized she'd sprayed it directly onto her clothes and thus would smell like a freshly groomed pooch for the rest of the day.

Peter watched her, frowning. "Look," he said in a booming voice. "I can tell you're freaked out that I hit a woman. I'm ashamed of my actions. I shouldn't have done it, and I'm sorry I did. But, you know, Millicent provoked me, and I'll bet she crossed the line with someone else too." He paused. "She probably deserved what happened to her."

Shannon felt repulsion for the man snake through her, but she kept a straight face. "If you think Millicent deserved to die, then she must have done something horrific to you."

"She trash-talked my little Maddy." He picked up his fluffy fur ball of a dog and cuddled her near his neck. "No one talks about you like that, do they, Maddy-pooh?" His voice shifted to a creepy, high-pitched baby talk. "This little girl's a champion, and when I'm allowed back on the circuit, we'll prove it."

"So ... to confirm, you think because Millicent said unkind words about your dog, she deserved to die."

Peter shrugged. "Eye for an eye."

Shannon thought that if ever the term "barking mad" should be applied to anyone, it was Peter Needlemeyer. She gripped the canister at her side more tightly. "Would you mind telling me where you were between five and seven last night?"

"At the inn, having dinner." His defensive gaze met hers. "Alone."

"For two hours?"

"Maybe an hour for dinner, but after that, I spent a few

hours in the lobby, shooting the breeze with other dog owners." He took a step toward Shannon, and she took a step back.

"Is there anyone who can confirm that you were there?" she pressed.

He laughed. "Look at me. The waitress is bound to remember me, and if she doesn't, then I paid with a credit card. I don't remember who all I talked to in the lobby, but the uptight owner of the inn kept glaring at me like I was making too much noise, so ask him."

Shannon knew he was referring to Betty's husband, Tom. She would ask Tom about Mr. Needlemeyer as soon as possible. For the moment, she feared she'd pressed her luck far enough. "Thanks for your time, Mr. Needlemeyer."

"Say bye-bye to the nice lady, Maddy." Peter lifted his dog's front paw and waved it.

Unable to stomach the man's bizarre behavior for a moment longer, Shannon hurried into the crowd. She ditched the canister and sat down on a bench to regroup. Digging out her notepad, she crossed Gus Krause's name off her suspect list and made a note to talk to Tom about Peter as soon as possible—not that there was any chance she'd forget. She looked up and caught Peter watching her. His eyes glazed in a creepy stare. He was the perfect suspect—emotionally unstable, spiteful, and strong as an ox. He could easily crack Millicent's skull with a trophy.

But he claimed to have an alibi.

If his alibi panned out, that would leave Lilly Lansdown and Cassandra Presley as Shannon's only suspects. Until she could talk with Tom, she'd make the best use of her time and focus on them. Looking at the dog show schedule, she noticed that Cassandra's poodle was scheduled to show within the hour, so she would no doubt be in the grooming tent.

Careful to avoid any further eye contact with Peter, Shannon made her way toward the tent. Kate stood outside the entrance with her trusty clipboard in hand.

"I didn't expect to see you here," Shannon said as she approached.

Kate wrinkled her nose. "Why do you smell like oranges and a baby's bum?"

"Because grooming spray doesn't make a good weapon."

"What?"

Shannon sighed. "It's a long story. Why aren't you at your booth?"

"Another volunteer didn't show up for this post, so I got Tina to cover my booth." Kate removed a business card from the clipboard and handed it to Shannon. "I stopped by my shop and got the contact information for Millicent's attorney. This is the guy she used to sue me."

Shannon read the card. "Attorney Charles Greer. I've seen his commercials on television."

Kate snorted. "Leave it to Millicent to hire a lawyer who hawks his services on TV. She probably thought she'd get a deal."

Shannon pocketed the card. "I was hoping to catch Cassandra Presley in there. Do you know if she's inside the tent?"

Kate tapped her clipboard. "I checked her in a few minutes ago."

"You're sure?"

Kate nodded. "I remembered her name from your suspect list, and I kept my eye out for her."

"Could you point her out?"

"Sure. Follow me." Kate stepped into the tent, and Shannon followed.

Feeling ten degrees warmer from the sun beating down on the fabric, the air inside the tent was stifling. Shannon stopped in front of one of the large fans and waited for Kate to point out Cassandra.

"She's the bleached blonde in the red shirt, first row," Kate said.

Shannon spotted Cassandra fussing over a black poodle. *The woman I saw Grayson talking to earlier.* Dressed in a business suit, her face glistened from the heat. "It's odd that she's wearing a suit in this heat."

"Dog show rules require owners to dress formally while in the show ring, but it is strange that she has the jacket on right now."

"Hiding a bite mark perhaps?" Shannon mused and then gathered her nerve to confront another suspect. "Wish me luck."

"Of course. Good luck—and thank you," Kate said. Then she headed back outside.

Shannon pulled her notepad out to fan her face and scanned the room. Blow dryers hummed from many of the stations, and owners chatted loudly over the noise.

Shannon approached the willowy blonde as she ran a brush through her poodle's curly hair. "Cassandra?"

The woman looked up. "Yes?"

"I wondered if I might talk to you about Millicent Downing."

Cassandra dropped the brush and grabbed Shannon's arm. "Is this about Scarlet? Did you find her? Is she OK?"

"No, she hasn't been found." Shannon extricated herself and stepped back.

"Oh, no, that's terrible." Cassandra dropped onto a wooden stool and stroked her dog's head. "I can't imagine what I'd do if someone took my Fifi."

Shannon studied the woman. She was the only owner who'd asked about Scarlet, and she seemed genuinely upset. "I'm sure Scarlet will be found safe and sound."

"Yes, that's what we have to believe." Cassandra fanned her face, then pushed up her jacket sleeves.

As she did, Shannon spotted an angry circular wound on Cassandra's forearm that very much resembled a bite mark.

"You've been bitten." Shannon pointed at the injury. "That must have hurt."

"It's nothing." Cassandra quickly pulled down her sleeve.

"Did Fifi bite you?"

"Of course not." Cassandra eyed Shannon suspiciously. "You never mentioned your name."

"Shannon McClain. I'm Kate Ellis's friend."

Cassandra furrowed her brows. "I'm not sure I know a Kate Ellis."

"She's the one taking names at the entrance." Fearing Cassandra had become too suspicious and would stop talking, Shannon quickly changed the subject. "How are you enjoying your stay with us in Apple Grove?"

Cassandra settled back on her stool. "I love the ocean. Fifi and I went for a nice long walk on the beach last night."

"Nothing like watching the sun set on the horizon. Did

you stay out late enough to catch it?" Shannon asked.

"No." Cassandra patted Fifi's head. "My little Fifi got so dirty, we couldn't stay until sunset. I had to give her a bath and make sure she got plenty of rest for today's show."

"Are you staying at the inn?"

"Yes, but considering all the dog shows we attend, I should probably get an RV." Cassandra stroked Fifi's curly coat. "Shouldn't I, girl?"

"Five minutes, people," a big burly man shouted from the end of the row.

Cassandra picked up Fifi. "If you'll excuse me, we're on."

"Good luck." Shannon scooted out of the way.

With all the owners kicking into high gear in their final preparations, Shannon knew she wouldn't be able to talk with anyone else, so she headed toward the exit. She found Kate still rooted in the same spot outside the entrance.

"Well?" Kate asked.

Shannon quickly relayed the conversation. "If Cassandra was the one to take Scarlet, do you think Scarlet would bite her?" she asked.

Kate considered the question. "Scarlet's never been a biter, but she would likely have felt threatened after Millicent was attacked. I think it's possible she could've snapped in a situation like that, especially if a stranger tried to pick her up."

"Then I think it would be a good idea to keep an eye on Cassandra for the rest of the afternoon. How long will this round of judging take?"

Kate glanced at her schedule. "It's scheduled to last an hour, but it wouldn't be unusual for the session to run long."

"Would you mind calling me when it ends? I'd like to go find Coleen and make sure she's behaving herself."

Kate laughed. "You don't think she is?"

"I think it's highly improbable."

"Congratulations on the big date, by the way." Kate winked. "Michael is quite a catch. If I were a little bit older—"

"Please. Everyone is making too much of this. I have *not* 'caught' him, and he is not a fish."

"OK, have it your way, but the way he's staring at you right now says otherwise—that he's taking you on a date, I mean. Not that he's a fish."

"Huh?" Shannon turned to follow Kate's gaze.

Michael leaned against a tree, his ankles crossed. He offered a small wave when their eyes met, and Shannon felt the usual blush rising up her neck.

"Aren't you at least going to go say hi?" Kate asked.

"Yes. Of course," Shannon said, but she hesitated to move. *Why do I feel this way? Just because he asked me to accompany him to a work function, it should not make things weird between us.*

She waited for a rowdy group of teens to pass and then crossed the sidewalk. "Are you enjoying the dog show?" she asked him, forcing a smile to hide her nervousness.

"Honestly?"

"Yes."

"Then no." He smiled. "I'm not a big dog lover, but I do enjoy watching people."

The way he looked at her made her feel like his words held a double meaning. He enjoyed watching people, but he particularly enjoyed watching her. *Could that be true?*

As she stepped closer, she noticed his nose wrinkle ever so slightly, a brief flash of confusion cross his face.

"Sorry about the smell," she said, fighting the urge to giggle at his expression. "I don't usually wear grooming spray as perfume. I'm hoping it will dissipate soon."

"It's ... strong." He leaned in closer to sniff. "You smell like a fruity poodle and ... something else."

Shannon chuckled. "Such flattery."

"Sorry." He tried to look sincere. "What I meant to say is, are you planning to wear that lovely scent on Saturday night? If so, how would you feel about us driving to dinner in a convertible—with the top down?"

She gave him a playful swat. "I'm glad you brought that up. I've been meaning to talk to you about Saturday night."

His forehead creased. "Ah, so that explains it."

"Explains what?"

"Coleen's unending comments about Saturday night." He pushed away from the tree looking like he wanted to flee. "You don't want to go, and she was trying to subtly let me down. It's OK, really."

Shannon snorted. "Subtle and Coleen do not go together in the same sentence. And I do still want to go."

"Then what's she been hinting around at all morning?"

"With Coleen, it's hard to tell. But *I'd* like to know how formal the event is, so I know what to wear."

"Oh ... right. I'm sorry I didn't think to mention that." He smiled broadly. "The hotel is dressy, but it's not a black-tie affair."

"That's fortunate," she said, "because my tux is at the cleaners."

He laughed, and the tension between them evaporated. "Can I pick you up at five-thirty? The dinner starts at seven. Since I'm one of the hosts, I want to allow time for traffic in Portland."

"That will be fine."

Michael's expression turned contemplative as he stared over her head.

"I suppose Grayson told you he still considers Kate a viable suspect in Millicent's murder," she said.

Michael nodded. "He mentioned that she doesn't have an alibi, and she might have motive from an old lawsuit. Plus, everyone in town has heard Eloise White's story about Kate wanting to take Scarlet away from Millicent."

"I'll admit the evidence seems to be mounting against her, but I can't believe Kate would be a part of something like this." Shannon sighed in exasperation. "I saw someone flee the scene—and it wasn't Kate."

"If Kate's innocent, Grayson will eventually figure that out."

"But meanwhile, she—and her business—will suffer."

"Kate's not his only suspect."

Shannon knew better than to ask Michael for details he couldn't offer. "I gave Grayson the names of my suspects. I saw him talking to one of them. I hope he follows up on the others too."

"I'm sure he will. He'll probably never admit it to you, but he knows you're good at identifying potential suspects."

She smiled. "Thanks for telling me that. I never would've guessed he felt that way. By the way, I learned the name of my mystery man from the nurse's station. It's Peter Needlemeyer.

Would you believe he actually hit Millicent a year ago?"

Michael frowned. "He physically assaulted her?"

"Yes." Shannon relayed Peter's justification for his actions and how he claimed Millicent had egged him on.

"That's no excuse to hit anyone—much less a woman." Michael's frown deepened. "I don't like the idea of him anywhere near you."

"Trust me, I have no plans to be alone with the man. If I need to talk to him again, I'll make sure it's in a well-lit public place."

"Even better, make sure I'm with you."

Shannon's heart sped up at the fervency behind his words, and she smiled up at him. He returned the smile, and suddenly she felt self-conscious. "I should go find Coleen before she gets into more trouble."

"I'm sure you're already too late," he teased, his expression softening. "She may be a nut, but you're lucky to have such a good friend."

"That I am," Shannon said, wishing Coleen didn't live halfway across the world from her—even if she did want to wring her dear friend's neck on occasion. "I'll see you later."

She turned to leave, but Michael caught her by the hand.

"I meant what I said about Peter," he warned. "Don't tangle with a man like that alone. He might snap, and there's no telling what he'd do. I'll make sure Grayson's got him on his radar, but you call me if you plan to speak to him again. OK?"

Shannon nodded, the warmth from his hand threatening to melt her senses.

"And one more thing ..." He hesitated, as if searching for the right words.

"What is it?"

He sniffed the air with a grimace. "I meant what I said earlier about the convertible." A slow, devilish grin spread across his face.

"Bounder," Shannon shot back, feeling a smile tug at the corners of her lips. She pulled her hand free from his grasp, raised her chin, and turned and walked away.

— 10 —

After following Cassandra all afternoon to no avail, Shannon shared a pizza, delivered by the local pizza parlor, with Coleen and Kate. They relaxed in Espresso Yourself's soft leather chairs and spent the better part of an hour eating and getting caught up on all the news from back home with Coleen.

After polishing off her third slice, Kate groaned and set down her plate. She eyed the pizza box. "I didn't realize how hungry I was. The rest is yours, girls."

"Not if I hope to keep my girlish figure," Shannon said. "I'll put it in the refrigerator, and we can snack on it later."

Coleen's hand shot out. "Not so fast. My girlish figure has been missing for years, and I don't care. I'd like another slice."

Shannon chuckled and pulled her hands away from the pizza. "It's all yours."

Kate looked at her watch. "As much as I'd like to stay and chat, I should be getting back to my booth."

"Would you mind looking at the pictures from Millicent's house before you go?" Shannon asked. "I think we've put it off long enough."

Kate's forehead creased. "I guess not. If you think it will be of help."

"It might be. I know it's hard to see the crime scene again, but I'm hoping you'll spot something I've missed." Shannon retrieved the photos from her tote bag. She handed the first one to Kate and pointed at the blank spot on the wall. "I'm wondering if our killer took whatever was hanging here."

Kate shook her head, her ponytail swinging. "Millicent took it down. It was a certificate Scarlet received at the Doggie Delights show last year. Scarlet placed in the rankings but didn't win. Since Scarlet won this year, Millicent didn't think she needed to keep the 'losing' certificate posted."

Shannon flipped to the next picture with the empty place on the bookcase. "And what about this spot? I can tell from the dust pattern that something sat there not too long ago."

Kate studied the picture, a quizzical look on her face. "I'm not sure about this one. Maybe if you enlarge the picture I can read the engraving on the trophies nearby and figure it out."

"I'll enlarge it tonight." Shannon flipped through the other pictures, and they discussed them, but Kate didn't notice anything unusual.

Coleen held out her hand. "Let me give them a go in case I see something you both missed."

Kate's cellphone chirped from her pocket. Her brow furrowed as she looked at the screen. "I have to take this. It's Tina. She might need my help at the booth."

As Kate's side of the conversation played out, it became clear that Tina did indeed require help.

Sighing, Kate hung up. "Tina needs me to replenish the cash box."

Shannon pointed at the pictures. "Will you take the pictures with you and give them a more thorough look?"

"Sure." Kate stood. Coleen handed her the pictures, and she tucked them in her backpack. "I'll see you both later."

"Let me put the pizza away, and we'll walk out with you." Shannon got up and grabbed the pizza box.

Groaning, Coleen slowly came to her feet. "I shouldn't have had that last slice. Don't say 'I told you so.'"

"Wouldn't dream of it," Shannon said as she stored the pizza and then followed Kate and Coleen out of the shop.

"FYI," Shannon said, "I called Millicent's lawyer this afternoon, but I had to leave a message on his voice mail. With any luck, he'll call back soon."

Kate shouldered her backpack. "Since it's the weekend and all, do you really think he'll return your call?"

"We can hope." Shannon offered a comforting smile as she locked the door. "Keep the faith, sweetie. We'll resolve this mess somehow."

"Thank you. I'm trying to stay positive." Kate's lips tipped in the faintest of smiles, then she spun and headed for Ultimutt Grooming to retrieve the needed cash.

Shannon and Coleen weaved their way through the thick evening crowd. They approached the shelter booth where a man Shannon didn't know waved at them. Shannon assumed he was the dog owner who'd filled in for the missing volunteer.

Coleen waved back. "That's Oliver Daniels. I met him this afternoon. Let me introduce you." She grabbed Shannon's hand and pulled her over to the booth. "Oliver, I'd like you to meet the good friend I was telling you about earlier. "

Shannon took in the tall, well-built man's appearance and held out her hand. "I'm Shannon McClain."

"Oliver Daniels." His warm green eyes settled on her face. "I've heard a lot about you—all good, of course."

"It's kind of you to staff the booth when we're short-handed."

A genuine smile lit his face. "Anything to help save homeless animals."

Shannon caught him glancing at her ring finger. "Coleen, can I talk to you a minute?" She grabbed Coleen by the sleeve and pulled her away from the table.

"You look upset. Is something wrong?" Coleen asked, eyes wide.

"Are you trying to fix me up with that guy? Did you lead him to believe I'm looking for a date?"

Coleen snorted. "Of course not. You're dating Michael." Her focus shifted to Oliver. "But now that you mention it, if things don't work out with Michael, Oliver is quite handsome, and he's an attorney, so he *would* be a great catch."

Shannon stifled a groan. "Come on. I'm keeping you in my sight." She pulled Coleen further away from the booth.

"See you later, Oliver," Coleen called out.

As they walked away, Shannon could feel him watching them, and she hoped Coleen hadn't inadvertently led him to think she was looking for someone to date. They slipped behind the Espresso Yourself table, and after Essie departed, they both worked furiously to keep up with the evening crowd.

Business was so good that Shannon had to return to the coffee shop in the craft market several times for supplies, and by the time the sun cast brilliant reds and oranges over the park, she was thoroughly exhausted. She dropped onto a chair next to Coleen.

"I forgot how tiring volunteering at events like this can be." Shannon rolled her neck to loosen kinks from the long day.

Coleen sat forward. "Speaking of volunteers, I'm supposed to tell whoever is in charge of the schedule for the shelter's booth that Oliver will volunteer again tomorrow if he's needed."

"Oliver?" Shannon asked.

Coleen frowned. "Och, you *are* tired. He's the man I introduced you to at the shelter's booth. The one you accused me of trying to set you up with, remember?"

"Oh, right."

"You know, I had the best time talking to him. He has tons of interesting stories." Coleen settled back in her chair, stretched her arms over her head, and yawned.

"I'm not the tired one. You are." Shannon cast an appraising look at her friend. "Jet lag is getting to you."

"Aye. That it is. A teensy bit of a rest, and I'll be ready to help you close up the booth." Coleen's eyelids drifted closed.

Shannon heard voices approach and peered down the sidewalk, where Michael strolled next to Melanie, Betty, and Joyce. They moved at a leisurely pace. Their long day appeared to have taken a toll on them too.

At the sound of their voices, Coleen's eyes suddenly flew open, and she followed Shannon's gaze. "Here comes Michael," she announced, as if he were the only person in the group.

Expecting that she looked as tired as her friends, Shannon ran a hand over her hair and cast Coleen a warning glance. "Whatever you're thinking about saying or doing, please don't."

"I wasn't," Coleen said innocently as she stood. "Anyway, I'm too tired to be ornery."

When the Purls reached the booth, Shannon asked, "Would one of you be able to give Coleen a ride home? I still have an hour or so of cleanup to do here, and jet lag has gotten the best of her."

"I'll be glad to," Melanie offered.

"Thanks, Mel." Shannon took Coleen by the arm, urging her toward Melanie—and away from Michael.

"Oh, you poor thing." Melanie took Coleen's arm. "We can leave right away." The two of them said their goodbyes and set off for Melanie's car.

"Betty," Shannon said, facing her friend, "when you get home, will you ask Tom if he remembers a tall, bald man hanging out in the lobby last night after dinner? At least until seven?"

Betty perked up. "Sure. Is this guy a suspect?"

"As far as I'm concerned, he sure is. His name is Peter Needlemeyer."

"I'll ask Tom about it the minute I get home, which can't come soon enough for me." She linked her arm with Joyce's. "We should get going, or I'll be dragging in the morning."

Shannon said goodbye to her friends, and as she turned back to Michael, she caught sight of Grayson standing a short distance away. Hidden in the shadows near a tree, his keen eyes watched Kate as she secured the flap on the main show tent.

"I wonder what he's up to?" Shannon mused.

Michael followed her gaze. "You mean Grayson?"

"M-hm. He appears to be spying on Kate."

"It's not unusual for an officer to keep an eye on a suspect." He paused. "Nor is it illegal."

Shannon nodded. "And neither is taking a stroll about

the park. I'll be right back." She darted away, heading straight toward Grayson.

"Shannon, wait," Michael called after her, but she kept going.

She joined Grayson near the tree, stopping to stand directly in front of him, partially blocking his view of Kate. "Hello, Chief. Lovely evening, isn't it?"

Grayson casually shifted his weight to look around Shannon's full head of hair. "I suppose."

"Couldn't have asked for better weather for the show." Shannon leaned to the side and smiled, blocking his view again. "The turnout was better than we'd hoped for."

The chief grunted in response as he moved to the other side.

Shannon mirrored his movements, eliciting a scowl from Grayson. "Is something going on over there?" she asked innocently.

Grayson sighed, "Yes. And if you keep this nonsense up much longer, I'll arrest you for obstructing justice."

"Oh my, what am I obstructing?"

Grayson eyed her for a moment. "I'm following up on a theory from the medical examiner in hopes of ruling out your friend. I don't want Kate to be guilty any more than you do—she's one of our own."

"I like the sound of that. What's the theory?" Shannon asked as Michael came to stand beside her.

"The angle of Millicent's head injury indicates that the killer is right-handed and taller than Millicent," Grayson said. "I could rule out Kate if she's left-handed."

Shannon was careful to keep her expression neutral.

Not only was Kate taller than Millicent, she was also right-handed. Those facts would only further lodge Kate at the top of Grayson's suspect list.

"I see. Have you had a chance to talk to the suspects I mentioned earlier?" Shannon asked.

"I have." He paused. "Gus checks out."

"Since you didn't mention Lilly, can I assume she's still a viable suspect?"

"You could assume that."

"OK ..." Shannon paused. "I saw you talking to Cassandra Presley."

"Yes."

"You should know I've learned she had an altercation with Millicent. I saw a bite mark on her arm too. If Scarlet bit her, it could be Cassandra's blood that was found near Scarlet's crate in Millicent's house."

Grayson quirked a brow. "Could be."

"And you can add the name Peter Needlemeyer to the list of people you should talk to."

"I filled Grayson in on Needlemeyer after you told me about your run-in with him," Michael interjected.

Grayson nodded. "I'm on the lookout for him."

"Good," Shannon said. "He clearly has some anger management issues."

"Yes, and I strongly advise you steer clear of him," Grayson warned. "Now, I appreciate all of these tips, Shannon, but if you wouldn't mind, I'd like to speak with Michael alone and then get back to business here."

Shannon looked from Grayson to Michael. "Of course. Good night."

"See you tomorrow," Michael said, a gleam in his eye.

Though she was frustrated, Shannon forced a smile. It wasn't Michael's fault that Kate happened to be right-handed and taller than Millicent. But why did the deck seem to be stacking higher against Kate with each passing hour?

Residual frustration fueled Shannon with energy, and she packed up her belongings in record time. She secured her booth, then grabbed her personal items and crossed the street to the Paisley Craft Market. Inside the shop, she put her aggravation to work, cleaning and straightening. She finished in fifteen minutes what usually took thirty and snapped off the shop's lights.

Outside, she glanced at the park, now dark and lifeless. Kate had obviously finished securing the tent and turned off the lights on her way out. Shannon locked the shop door and then headed toward her old truck, the only vehicle still parked on the street.

The usual nighttime fog had settled over Apple Grove, shrouding the town in a hazy blanket. As she walked down the sidewalk, an uneasy feeling replaced her anger, and she stopped to survey the area.

Half expecting to see Peter Needlemeyer lying in wait, she nervously scanned the shadows clinging to the buildings and the darkened park. Nothing moved except for the tree branches swaying in the light breeze. Still, an ominous feeling gripped her like a garrote, and she quickened her pace toward Old Blue.

Her mind whirled with a vision of Peter's massive feet pounding behind her. More and more, it seemed like he might be the killer. She remembered him using his right hand to accept the box of bandages from the nurse, and he was more than tall enough to fit the medical examiner's criteria. His muscular arms could easily wield a makeshift weapon with enough force to do damage.

Fear cut a path through her heart, and she moved even faster, practically running for her truck.

Nearing the vehicle, she spotted a yellow piece of paper tucked under her windshield wiper. Glancing behind her, she quickly plucked it from under the wiper and flipped it open. Bright letters cut from a magazine were pasted on the lined notepaper.

MIND YOUR OWN BUSINESS ... OR YOU'LL PAY.

Her head shot up, and she searched the darkness for her foe. Fear—stark and vivid now—knotted her stomach. The warning proved she'd ruffled somebody's feathers, which meant her investigation was on the right track.

A rustling at the street corner broke the silence. The sound of receding footsteps reverberated off the sidewalk. The sharp footfalls trailed down the side street, each retort vanishing into the misty air as quickly as it rang out.

Without thinking, Shannon charged down the sidewalk, following the sound. She rounded the corner and scoured the area, her breath coming in short wisps in the cooler air.

Farther down the street, a figure disappeared into the swirly fog like a whisper of her imagination. Craning her neck, she couldn't tell if the person was a man or woman, much less determine the person's identity.

But whoever it was made it perfectly clear that he—or she—knew hers.

— 11 —

Shannon stood in the kitchen listening to the *drip, drip, drip* of the coffee as it filled the carafe. Desperately needing a morning caffeine jolt, she inhaled the aromatic scent and stifled a yawn. Fortunately, when she'd arrived home the previous night, Coleen had already gone to bed, allowing Shannon to tumble into hers too. And despite the dire warning left on her truck's windshield, she'd slept soundly until her alarm pulled her out of bed.

Footsteps padded down the hallway, and Coleen entered the room. She settled a hand on her hip. "Why didn't you wake me last night?"

"I got home later than I thought I would, and I was too tired to talk."

"You seem tense. Did something happen?" Coleen picked up the teakettle but kept her eyes on Shannon.

"I had a little problem last night." As the coffeepot gurgled its readiness, Shannon told Coleen about the note.

"Oh, you poor thing." Coleen said. "This is getting too dangerous. I know you won't want to hear this, but perhaps you should heed the warning."

"But the warning clearly means I'm getting close to solving this." Shannon filled her mug with rich, black coffee. "I don't want to give up now."

Coleen shuddered. "I hate to think of you finding that

note all by yourself."

"Me too. Let's change the subject for a bit."

"Agreed," Coleen said. "Are you looking forward to tonight?"

"Dinner with Michael? Sure."

Coleen frowned. "You don't really sound like you mean it."

"You know this whole dating thing has me flustered."

"You're afraid of putting yourself out there. Of getting hurt." Coleen sat on the opposite side of the island.

Shannon shrugged. "Maybe, but I think it has more to do with the fact that I feel like I'm cheating on John."

"I've never been in your shoes, but I'm guessing that's a natural feeling. But, honey, John would be the first to tell you to move on."

Shannon sipped her coffee. "You're right, I suppose."

"But?"

"But I still don't know if I'm ready. I mean, dating? I haven't done that for more years than I care to count."

"I know you," Coleen said. "You're ready. Relax and enjoy the night with Michael. No expectations. Just a fun night out."

Shannon pulled in a breath. "A fun and relaxing night out—like I would have with any of my friends."

"Maybe not *that* relaxed." Coleen's laughter bubbled over. "Let's go search your closet for a knock-him-dead outfit worthy of your dating debut."

Shannon shook her head. "No need. I've already decided on the black dress I wore to your anniversary party."

Coleen wrinkled her nose. "It's awfully long."

"It barely covers my knees!"

"Precisely." Coleen tapped a finger on her chin. "I'm not sure it's the *right* dress to put a gleam in Michael's eyes."

"Gleaming eyes are not part of 'relaxing' and 'no expectations.'" Shannon finished her coffee and stood. "I need to spend some time on the computer before we go to the park."

"Way to change the subject."

Shannon rested her hands on her friend's shoulders. "I've got lots to do today. If I don't get this done now, I'll be rushing around this afternoon to fit everything in."

"On second thought, good idea to get it finished now." Coleen winked. "That way, you'll have plenty of time left in your day to primp before your date."

Shannon laughed. "Has anyone ever told you you're as tenacious as a pit bull?"

"Not today." Coleen's laughter mixed with the shrill whistle of the teapot.

As Coleen rose to turn it off, Shannon refilled her mug. "If you want to join me in the study, you'll have to promise to stop talking about Michael so I can focus."

"I promise," she said with a wink. "I'll fix my tea and be right in."

Shaking her head, Shannon strolled down the hallway. As much as Coleen was driving her to distraction, she was thrilled to have her best friend in town again. She only hoped she could find Millicent's killer soon so she could devote more attention to her friend before Coleen had to return to Scotland.

Shannon sat at her computer and responded to a few vital emails before enlarging and printing the photo of the shelf in Millicent's den for Kate.

"What are you working on?" Coleen asked, startling Shannon.

Shannon put the photo in her bag and opened the

Internet. "I'm looking for any information on my three suspects, starting with Cassandra."

"Let me know when you find something interesting." Coleen sank into an overstuffed chair covered with a pale yellow slipcover.

Shannon entered "Cassandra Presley" in the search engine and narrowed the results by state. She read two dog show articles but found nothing that would give Cassandra an obvious motive to murder Millicent. Shannon followed the same procedure for Lilly and Peter and received the same kind of results.

Frustrated, she sat back. "I tried all three names. Nothing out of the ordinary turns up."

"Why don't you search for Millicent instead?"

"Good idea. I looked for information on her family yesterday, but I haven't searched for her." Shannon entered Millicent's name followed by "Apple Grove, Oregon." Several results hinted at a lawsuit filed against Millicent.

Shannon clicked on the first link. A hit turned up from the previous month.

"Coleen, you're a genius! Listen to this. Last month, Millicent's neighbor, Rex Carrolton, filed a lawsuit against her for destroying his lawn. As Apple Grove's longstanding Yard of the Year contest winner, it seems he took great pride in it. He claims Scarlet started doing her business on his lawn, killing his grass and costing him this year's title. He'd failed to talk Millicent into controlling Scarlet, so he sued for the damages to his property and for defamation of character."

"Interesting." Coleen set down her mug and came to

stand behind Shannon. She scooted her chair to the side, giving her friend access to the full story.

As Shannon waited for Coleen to finish reading, she sipped her coffee and pondered Rex's claims.

Coleen *tsked* and leaned back. "Wow, he had nothing good to say about her, now did he?"

"No, but they'd lived next to each other for years before this suit was filed. So what happened to make Millicent refuse to keep Scarlet off his lawn?"

"Maybe Rex is a nasty neighbor, and Millicent finally had enough. She got back at him with Scarlet."

"That sounds possible, I suppose, though would someone—even someone as adversarial as Millicent—risk letting her dog run free?" Shannon asked.

"Who says the dog had to run free? Rex couldn't stand watch over his yard all day. If Millicent was doing this on purpose, she could've easily taken Scarlet out on her leash when he wasn't home or in the middle of the night when he was sleeping."

"Good point."

"Even so, is it worth killing someone over?"

Shannon scoffed. "Is anything?"

Coleen lifted her face to the ceiling and rested a finger on her chin. Shannon recognized the position as Coleen's "thinking pose." Shannon had witnessed the same stance so many times, she knew better than to interrupt before Coleen was ready to talk.

"Why haven't we heard anything about this?" Coleen finally asked. "I would think if it was that big of a deal, someone would have mentioned it by now."

"I guess it's because everyone was focused on the dog show. And I hate to admit it, but that included me. Since Millicent was murdered this weekend, I assumed her death was related to the show, and I didn't look closely at the locals." Shannon sighed. "I'm as guilty as Grayson of wearing blinders about suspects."

Coleen shook her head. "Don't be so hard on yourself. Kate knows you're doing your best to help."

"Thanks," Shannon said, doubt lingering inside. "But I plan to rectify my mistake today."

She clicked on the next article, a local news story about Rex losing the yard contest for the first time in five years. The attached picture showed Rex staring at his lawn. Lush and green, it was dotted with yellowed and brown circular spots—likely caused by a dog.

"He must have hated Scarlet," Shannon said, looking up at Coleen. "If he knew Millicent was out of town, he might've gone to the house intending to kidnap Scarlet so she couldn't ruin his lawn anymore—"

"But Millicent returned home unexpectedly and caught him in the act!" Coleen finished, excitement pulsing in her voice.

"Exactly. Then he panicked and hit her with the first thing he could grab."

"Sounds plausible to me."

"Not only plausible," Shannon said as she rose, "but an excellent lead. I intend to pay Mr. Carrolton a visit before I go to the park. Care to join me?"

Coleen took a sip of her tea. "I wouldn't miss it."

— 12 —

Shannon parked her truck along the curb in front of Rex Carrolton's address. "Nice neighborhood."

Coleen, nearly comatose on the ride over, peered out her window. "I'll say."

Shannon looked around at the street. The homes all sat on large lots with plenty of space between neighbors. Yellow crime scene tape circled Millicent's one-story house, which was modest in comparison to Rex's home. His home boasted two-story glass windows in the front, and Shannon could see through the home to the swells of the ocean beyond. It sat on a large corner lot, and flowering perennials ringed his yard. The lush grass was immaculately groomed—except for the smattering of yellow and brown spots.

"That must be Rex," Shannon said, pointing at the hook-nosed man in the front yard. He whistled as he dug out a large brown patch from the lawn. "He's tall."

"And he appears to be right-handed."

"He fits the medical examiner's criteria for the murderer." Shannon pulled her keys from the ignition.

An uneasy look swept over Coleen's face. "The threatening note on your windshield—if he did kill Millicent, maybe we shouldn't be here alone."

"Don't tell me. You want to call Michael."

Coleen's expression instantly cleared. "Now that you mention it, that's a great idea."

"But not one I'll entertain at the moment." Shannon opened her door, the rusty hinges protesting. "You can stay here if you want."

Coleen shook her head and grabbed her door handle. "Not a chance."

At the sound of slamming doors, Rex turned and watched them approach with a critical eye. His lips drew down in the same deep scowl Shannon had seen in the newspaper, nearly stopping her in her tracks.

"Are you *sure* you want to talk to him now?" Coleen said in her too-loud whisper.

"He does look intimidating."

Coleen edged closer to Shannon. "We could still call Michael."

For once, Shannon knew her friend wasn't trying to play matchmaker but was truly concerned for their safety.

"We'll be fine," Shannon assured her. "It's broad daylight on a public street."

"If you say so."

"Let me do the talking." Shannon walked up the cobblestone walkway lined with green hostas.

Rex lifted a hand over his eyes. "Can I help you ladies?"

"I hope so." Shannon smiled. "You're Rex Carrolton, correct?"

He eyed them with suspicion. "Yes."

"Brilliant. I was wondering if you might have a minute to talk about Millicent Downing."

His hand dropped. "Are you a reporter?"

"No. I'm just a friend trying to figure out what happened to her." Shannon felt a little guilty intimating that she was a friend of Millicent's when she meant she was Kate's friend, but she thought it wise not to go into detail. "Looks like you're having a problem with your lawn."

He smirked. "I was."

"What are those spots from? Grubs?"

"A dog that's not kept in its own yard." The venom in his voice gave Shannon a moment's pause.

She couldn't tell if he hated all dogs or just Scarlet in particular. "You wouldn't be talking about the missing Scarlet, would you?"

"I would. Good riddance to her and any dog that isn't properly restrained by its owner." His lip curled up in a snarl. "It was a happy day for me when she went missing."

Coleen clutched her chest and stepped back.

His cold demeanor made Shannon want to move back too, but she needed to finish questioning him. "Do you have any idea what happened to Scarlet?"

He appraised Shannon for a moment. "No."

His abbreviated answers were starting to irk her, but she wouldn't give up. "Were you home the night ... she went missing?"

"No." He paused. "I was working out at the senior center." He appeared fit, and Shannon could believe he worked out.

"Poor Millicent." Shannon covered her mouth with her hand, shaking her head. "I still can't believe something so horrible could happen in a nice neighborhood like this. Who would've thought?"

Coleen inched closer and put her arm around Shannon for effect. "There, there."

Rex merely grunted and turned his focus back to his digging.

"So you didn't see Millicent leave for her trip earlier that day or notice anything suspicious later?" Shannon asked him.

Rex didn't look up. "Nope."

"Were you aware Millicent was going out of town?"

"We weren't exactly on speaking terms after she blew a gasket over where I keep my a trash can, then allowed her dog to ruin my yard." He lifted his shovel and looked her in the eyes. "Now if you'll excuse me, I need to get back to my yard work."

"Preparing for the Yard of the Year contest, right?"

"Yep."

"You won that contest for five years straight with this amazing yard, if I'm not mistaken," Shannon rushed on, hoping a compliment would get him talking.

His eyebrows knit together. "And why would you know so much about me?"

Shannon searched for any answer other than she'd stalked him on the Internet, but excited barking from inside his house drew her attention away before she could come up with anything.

It sounded like the bark of a small dog.

"After the way you talked about dogs, I'm surprised you own one," Shannon remarked.

He didn't respond, and his blank expression gave nothing away.

She continued, "I love dogs, but I don't have one of my own. What kind of dog do you have?"

He sunk the shovel's blade into the loamy soil. "Anyone ever tell you to mind your own business?"

Shannon's mouth went dry. *Did Rex leave the note on my windshield?* "Quite recently, as a matter of fact."

"Might be a good idea for you to take that advice." He fixed her with a hard stare. "You ladies best be on your way."

"Come on." Coleen tugged on Shannon's arm and dragged her down the walk.

"That could be Scarlet inside, barking!" Shannon whispered.

At the sidewalk, Coleen dropped Shannon's arm. "Even if it is Scarlet, what are you going to do about it? You can't barge into his house uninvited. You're not a cop, and you can't get a search warrant. Besides, if he hated the dog so much, I doubt he'd keep her around."

"What if he intends to sell her under another name after all of this blows over? Even if he doesn't plan to harm her, I hate to leave without making sure that's not Scarlet in there."

Formulating a plan, Shannon glanced back at the house. Rex would surely spot them if they tried to sneak up from the side of the house and look in the windows. They could perhaps head down to the beach and approach from that angle, but with the large windows on both sides of his home, Rex was likely to see them regardless.

"I know that look, and I don't like it one bit," Coleen said. "What are you thinking?"

"That there are too many windows on that man's house. It would be impossible to look in without him seeing us."

"What if we asked the neighbors if he owns a dog? If they say yes, then we can assume it's his dog."

Shannon blinked. "Great idea. Come on." She rushed across the street, the sound of Coleen's sandals snapping close behind her. She strode up to the first house and pounded on the door.

A slight woman with gray hair opened the door a crack and peeked out. She didn't say a word but observed Shannon with the same distrust Rex had displayed. Shannon didn't blame her. She'd be wary too if a murder had been committed across the street from her home.

Shannon smiled broadly and introduced herself and Coleen. "I'm looking into Millicent's death for a friend of mine. You may know Kate from Ultimutt Grooming. She often takes care of Scarlet."

The woman offered a nervous smile. "Kate, yes. She's a lovely young woman. So respectful. Always cleaning up after Scarlet."

"Were you home the night Millicent was murdered?" Shannon asked, cringing at her bad transition.

The woman looked across the street and shuddered. "Thankfully, no. I was in Portland, visiting my daughter."

"Were you and Millicent friends?" Coleen asked.

The woman shook her head sadly. "As far as I know, Millicent didn't have any friends. At least not in the neighborhood, and I never saw anyone come to visit her except Kate."

"She wasn't friends with Rex Carrolton?"

"My word, no." The woman lowered her voice. "There's a long history of bad blood between them—most recently he took her to court over Scarlet ruining his lawn. Millicent, being the kind of woman she was, made sure Scarlet did her business in his lawn even more after that. Oh dear, I shouldn't gossip so. I fear I've said too much." She started to close the door.

Shannon stuck the toe of her shoe in it to keep the door from closing. "Wait! Please. I need to know if he owns a dog."

"Rex?" The woman chuckled. "Not likely. He hates all animals, even my cat, Bitsy."

Shannon and Coleen exchanged knowing looks. "One last question and then I promise we'll leave you in peace. Do you know if Rex ever works out at the senior center?"

The woman shook her head. "I invited him once. He says that's for old people like me. He claims he gets all the exercise he needs, working in his yard."

Rex lied.

Shannon offered the elderly woman a smile. "Thank you so much for your time. You've been a tremendous help."

The woman sighed, opening the door a few more inches. "I realize Kate won't come around now that Millicent's gone, but would you tell her I said hello, and that she's welcome to stop by and visit anytime she wants?" A hint of loneliness had crept into her words.

"Of course I'll tell her," Shannon said.

The woman closed the door, and her deadbolt clicked into place.

Shannon started down the walkway "After this murder is resolved, we need to bring that woman a plate of cookies— at the very least."

"That's a lovely idea."

"But first we need to prove Rex has Scarlet." Shannon stopped at the end of the walk and studied Rex's property.

He looked up from digging and met her gaze with a challenge.

"Look at him," Shannon whispered to Coleen. "It's almost as if he's daring me to come over."

"Really? That's what you're getting out of his evil glare?" Coleen's tone held a good measure of reproach. "You're just looking for an excuse to go over there again—and for the record, I think that's a bad idea."

"We need to get a look inside his house."

"But how?"

Shannon considered the possibilities. "You could distract him while I sneak around the side of the house and peek inside."

Coleen gulped. "What if a neighbor sees you? The last thing you need is to be arrested for peeping in windows. Chief Grayson would *not* go easy on you."

"You have a point." Shannon kept her eye on Rex, who'd returned to his digging.

"Why don't you call Grayson?" Coleen suggested. "He could request to see the dog."

"I don't know ..."

"Can you come up with a better idea?"

"Unfortunately, no." Shannon dug out her phone and pressed Grayson's icon. "But if this goes horribly wrong, I'm blaming you."

Grayson answered on the second ring. "Please don't tell me you found another body," he said before Shannon could offer a greeting.

"No, but I think I've found our missing dog." She filled him in on Rex Carrolton. "His neighbor was adamant that he hates dogs, but I'm sure I heard one barking inside his house."

"So? Maybe he's dog-sitting."

"Why would someone who hates dogs do that?"

Silence filled the phone. Shannon tapped her foot, waiting for him to say something.

"OK," he said finally. "I'll be right there. Try and stay out of trouble until I get there."

Shannon stowed her phone and turned to Coleen. "He's on his way. Let's wait in the truck."

"Good idea." Coleen wrinkled her nose. "That man is giving me the willies."

Rex kept his focus on them as they crossed the road and climbed into Old Blue. When she didn't start the engine and drive off, he planted his hands on the top of his shovel handle and glowered at her.

"Don't make eye contact with him," Coleen warned. "He reminds me of those dingoes you see in the wild—he's got their crazy eyes. Staring into them for too long might provoke him to attack."

Shannon snorted. "And when did you last encounter a wild dingo?"

"A few weeks ago." Coleen raised her chin. "On the television."

Shannon took one last look at the man whose expression screamed "killer" and felt a shiver run down her back. She hoped Grayson would show up quickly—before Rex turned feral and came after them with his shovel.

— 13 —

Shannon had expected to see Grayson's SUV come barreling down the street with its lights and siren blazing, but instead, it quietly inched along the road toward them as though Grayson were out for a Sunday drive. He parked on the opposite side of the road and casually climbed out of his vehicle. Settling his hat over his balding head, he gave the area a leisurely study.

"Goodness, I've never known the chief to move so slowly," Shannon said to Coleen as she pushed her door open. She hopped down from the truck and met Grayson by his vehicle.

"Hello, Shannon."

"Rex went back inside. He knows we heard a dog barking in his house. He's probably hiding Scarlet as we speak." Shannon's words tumbled out without pause.

Before Grayson could respond, Rex shot out of his front door. Grayson's focus shifted to the furious man as he stormed down the sidewalk, his hands pumping in step with each rapid stride.

"I suggest you ladies wait in your vehicle." Grayson said before crossing the road.

Seeing the wild look in Rex's eyes, Shannon was tempted to agree, but she didn't want to stand on the sidelines while Rex told tall tales to the chief. So she trailed after Grayson, and when she passed her truck, Coleen climbed out to join her.

"Don't tell me," Rex paused and stabbed a finger in Shannon's direction, "she called you and accused me of having something to do with Millicent's death."

"Now settle down, Rex," Grayson said calmly.

Rex fisted his hands. "You know I wasn't even home when Millicent was killed—"

"He claims he was at the senior center," Shannon interrupted, "but the woman across the street says he doesn't like the senior center because it's for old people."

A vein bulged in Rex's neck. "Tell this nosy redhead that she's all wrong and to mind her own business. Go ahead, Grayson. Tell her."

Grayson faced Shannon. "I just came from the senior center where I confirmed his alibi for the time of Millicent's death."

Shannon blinked. "But—"

"Not so smart now, are you, red?" Rex snarled.

Shannon couldn't believe she'd been so wrong about him. The wind evaporated from her sails, and she felt defeated.

Coleen took a step closer to Rex. "Maybe you didn't kill Millicent, but that doesn't mean you didn't take Scarlet."

"Yeah," Shannon added, suddenly feeling like an adolescent in a playground fight.

Rex shook his head in utter disbelief. "Shows what you know. I'd never want that yippy little dog."

"Maybe not as your pet, but you might kidnap her to keep her from using your yard again." Coleen crossed her arms.

"C'mon now, folks." Grayson stepped between them. "Let's stop flinging accusations at each other and talk this through. Do you have a dog inside, Rex?"

Rex kept his angry gaze locked on Shannon as he nodded. "My son had to go out of town. My grandson and his dog are here for the weekend."

Shannon saw a familiar exasperated look flash across Grayson's face. It usually meant he planned to lecture her about something later.

"Would you mind if we see the dog?" Grayson asked.

Rex tilted his chin at a defiant angle. "I would mind."

"Now, Rex," Grayson said. "Don't take an attitude with me. I'm sorry for this intrusion, but I can't leave until I see the dog."

"Fine. I'll get him." Rex spun and marched up his sidewalk.

The chief clamped a hand on the back of his neck and stared at Shannon. "I knew this wouldn't pan out. I should've listened to my intuition—and not you."

"It's Rex's fault," Coleen said. "If he'd been forthcoming, we wouldn't have needed to call you."

Grayson shifted his full attention to Coleen. "I know you, don't I?"

"We met earlier this year." Coleen smiled and held out her hand. "Coleen Douglas."

Grayson shook hands, but the wary expression remained on his face.

Coleen continued, "Please don't be mad at Shannon. I'm the one who convinced her to call you."

He sighed. "I suppose that's the preferable alternative

to her typical *modus operandi*. Lately she's been running around half-cocked, finding danger at every turn. Calling me is generally the *last* thing she thinks of doing."

Coleen gave a serious nod. "She can be that way sometimes."

"Hello, you two." Shannon planted her hands on her hips. "Remember me? I'm standing right here."

"Good," Grayson said. "Then there's a chance you're listening and might realize investigations are best left for law enforcement professionals."

Suddenly, Rex's front door jerked open and Grayson whirled, his hand drifting toward his gun. Rex, along with a boy around five years old, came jogging down the sidewalk behind a small, wiry terrier.

"This is my grandson, Andrew, and his dog, Max." Rex glared at Shannon. "Satisfied?"

Shannon stepped close to Grayson and lowered her voice to keep Andrew from hearing her doubts about his grandfather. "There could be another dog inside. You have to check."

"Mind if I take a look around inside, Rex?" Grayson asked.

"Of course I mind, but if it will get this nut off my sidewalk, then let's go." Rex spun on his heel.

"What about Max's walk, Grandpa?" Andrew asked, his face crestfallen.

"I'll be right back, and we can take Max then." He ruffled the boy's hair. "Stay in the yard until I come out."

Andrew nodded and knelt next to his dog. Guilt about coming between a grandfather and grandson niggled at Shannon.

"Max is a special dog," Coleen said cheerfully, and Shannon shot her friend a thankful look.

Andrew glanced up at Coleen. "You talk funny."

"I'm from Scotland. We all talk like this over there."

Andrew's eyes opened wide. "Wow. Is that another planet or something?"

Coleen laughed. "It's a lovely country way across the ocean."

"That's cool. Did you come here on a ship?"

"Sorry, no. I came on an airplane."

"Airplanes are cool." He glanced up at Shannon. "Are you from there too?"

"Yes, but Apple Grove is my home now."

He grinned, revealing a gap-tooth smile. "Do you want to play with Max and me?"

Shannon was about to agree when Grayson and Rex stepped outside. Shannon could tell by Grayson's irritated frown and Rex's smug look that there wasn't another dog inside.

"I'm sorry we bothered you, Rex." Grayson turned to Shannon. "A word," he said and strode toward his car.

"You might as well wait in the truck for me," she said to Coleen.

"Are you sure?"

"Yes. No sense in both of us getting yelled at." As Shannon trudged toward Grayson's SUV, she saw the woman across the street peering out of her window. Shannon waved, and she scuttled away.

Grayson stood by his opened door, his feet planted wide. "Are you happy now? You've embarrassed me and yourself."

"I'm really sorry," she said. "I didn't mean to put you in an embarrassing situation."

He glared at her. "You can bet I won't come running the next time you call."

"Not even if it's a life-or-death matter?" she squeaked.

"You mean like the night you thought you supposedly saw a man lurking around outside your house?"

She *had* seen someone, but she thought it best not to argue the point at that moment. "That or the threatening note that was left on my windshield last night."

Grayson frowned. "A note?"

"It told me to back off the investigation, or I'd pay the price."

He let out a sigh. "Do you still have it?"

She nodded. "In my truck."

"Get it."

She jogged to her truck, ignoring Rex's gloating expression as he passed by with his grandson and dog.

Shannon dug the note out of her glove box and returned to Grayson.

He studied the warning for only a moment then fixed his icy gaze on her again. "If something else like this happens in the future, you let me know *right away*." He slid behind the wheel and closed his door with a solid thump.

* * *

Shannon and Coleen traveled back to Main Street Park in silence. They parked and made their way toward Kate's table. With their unexpected trip to Rex's house delaying their arrival, the park had already swelled with visitors, and it took a concerted effort to wind through the crowd.

As they approached, Kate waved them over. "I'm glad you're here. The ladies could use some help at our charity table."

"You stay here and show the enlarged picture of Scarlet's trophy shelf to Kate," Coleen said. "I'll go help the Purls."

Shannon smiled her thanks and dug the photo from her bag.

Kate took the picture, holding it as if it were a snake that might bite her. She gazed at it and then tapped the trophy sitting by the empty spot. "This is from Scarlet's first major win. Millicent was happier than I'd ever seen her that day. She rushed out and bought a Lladro dog figurine."

"What in the world is a Lladro?"

"Lladro makes expensive porcelain collectibles." Kate's eyes narrowed. "Can I see the other picture of the shelf that has all the items on it?"

"Sure." Shannon dug in her bag until she located the photo in question.

Kate briefly looked at it, then slapped her forehead. "Of course, that's what's missing." She turned the picture to face Shannon. "See how there's a dog figurine next to every trophy? Every time Scarlet won, Millicent bought one to celebrate."

Shannon counted more than fifteen figurines in the picture. "Why would this one be missing?"

"I suppose since it's valuable, the killer could have taken it," Kate said. "But why take this one and not the others?" She continued to study the picture.

"If my theory that Millicent was killed because she surprised the killer is right," Shannon said, "it doesn't make sense that after he killed her, he would have the presence of mind to steal a figurine. Unless, of course, it was a random burglary gone wrong. But in that case, the killer would have taken more than one of these valuable pieces."

"I agree." Kate sighed. "It doesn't add up. Have you found anything else that can help?"

Shannon told Kate about the failed trip to Rex's house. "But don't lose hope. Lilly, Peter, and Cassandra are still viable leads. I'd like to learn more about Cassandra, so I'm going to keep an eye on her in case she slips up."

"Her dog placed yesterday, so she's probably hanging around the tent, sizing up the competition." Kate pulled out a revised schedule and flipped the page. "Now might be a good time to look for her."

"Then that's what I'll do."

On the way to the tent, Shannon dialed Millicent's attorney. His voice mail picked up again, and she sighed over her rotten luck. She left another message—this one more urgent—and hoped that he'd call back before day's end.

As Shannon neared the tent, she was fortunate enough to spot Cassandra coming out of it. She trailed the woman down the sidewalk, careful to keep a safe distance between them and stay hidden among the crowd. Cassandra's poodle strolled next to her, and every time she stopped, the poodle halted as well. Cassandra paused to talk with a lanky man, and Shannon stepped to the side to listen. They chatted about dog breeding and training, but Millicent's name never came up in the conversation. After a few minutes, Cassandra moved on, and Shannon trailed her down the main walkway.

Without warning, Cassandra spun. "I've already said all I'm going to say about Millicent, so you can stop following me." She glared at Shannon.

Shannon feigned innocence. "I beg your pardon?"

Cassandra planted a hand on her hip. "Drop the act. You've been tailing me since I came out of the tent."

The same irritation Shannon had felt at Rex's place bubbled to the surface. "OK, fine. You caught me. I do have one teensy additional question I wanted to ask you. Where were you when Millicent was killed?"

"It's none of your business." Cassandra picked up her dog and took off at a rapid clip.

Shannon doubted the woman would be running away if she didn't have something to hide.

"Two can play at that game," Shannon muttered and hurried to catch up.

Cassandra glanced over her shoulder, and when she saw Shannon closing the gap between them, she picked up speed. She plunged through the crowd, not bothering to stop or apologize when she rammed into people. Shannon at least offered an apologetic look, but she didn't stop either. She followed Cassandra as the woman scurried through the crowd.

Suddenly, a large dog darted in front of Shannon and growled at her. Seeing its bared teeth, Shannon froze in her tracks, afraid the dog might bite her.

"Sorry." The owner tugged her dog to the side. "He's tense with all the people around. Guess I'll take him home."

Shannon eased around the woman and scanned the crowd for Cassandra. She was nowhere in sight. Shannon continued through the crowd as fast as she could. Finally, she caught sight of Cassandra again in the clearing by the parking lot.

Cassandra settled her dog into a small car before jumping into the driver's seat.

Shannon sprinted across the lot, but by the time she got close enough to speak to Cassandra, the angry woman had revved her engine and backed out of the parking space. Shannon raised a hand as if she could stop the car, but Cassandra merely gave a snappy salute and sped out of the lot.

What are you hiding, Cassandra Presley?

— 14 —

Late in the afternoon, after Shannon had finished her responsibilities for her shop, she and Coleen headed to the grooming tent in search of Lilly Lansdown. Shannon had only an hour before she needed to go home and get ready for her night out with Michael, but she hoped to confirm Lilly's and Peter Needlemeyer's alibis before leaving for the day.

The oppressive heat hit Shannon in the face the moment she entered the tent.

"It feels like a sauna in here," Coleen said, fanning her hand in front of her face. "Do you see Lilly or Peter?"

"Lilly is the blonde standing by the tall brunette in the back of the tent. I recognize the brunette from yesterday; her name is Grace."

"I see them."

"Let's go." Shannon moved through the space, fanning herself with her program. She approached the plump blonde, who appeared bored. "Hello, Ms. Lansdown. Would you have a minute to answer a few questions?"

She peered at Shannon with a quizzical look. "Is this about my dog?"

"No. It's about Millicent Downing."

Lilly glanced uneasily at her friend and then back at Shannon. "What about her?"

"I heard that you had an altercation with her—"

"Whoa." Lilly held up a hand. "Before you accuse me of killing her, you should know I was having dinner at The Apple Grove Inn with Grace here when Millicent was killed. I've already told this to the police."

"That's right," Grace said. "We met in the dining room at five for cocktails."

"And your dinner lasted until seven?" Shannon asked.

"What can we say? It takes time to polish off a whole bottle of wine." Lilly looked at Grace, and the two of them started giggling.

Shannon was too hot and tired to find their laughter amusing. "Do you have any proof that you were at the inn?"

Lilly's laughter died, and a sour pucker claimed her lips. "You never said who you are and why this is any of your business."

"I'm sorry." Shannon smiled. "I'm Shannon McClain, and this is Coleen Douglas. We're both friends of Kate Ellis. She was the one who found Millicent, and the police suspect her of the murder. I'm trying to find out what *really* happened to Millicent."

Grace *tsked*. "Poor Kate."

Lilly nodded her agreement. "I'm more than willing to help Kate, but I'm not going to admit to a murder I didn't commit. I didn't kill Millicent." She pulled a receipt from her wallet. "I can't prove what time I arrived for dinner, but this shows the time I paid."

Shannon held up the receipt boasting a 7:15 p.m. time stamp. "Do you have any idea who wanted Millicent dead?"

"Gus Krause," Lilly and Grace said in unison and then laughed at their shared comment.

Shannon shook her head. "It wasn't Gus. He has an alibi."

"He's the only one I can think of." Lilly faced Grace. "Can you think of anyone else?"

"An easier question might be who *wouldn't* want to kill Millicent." Grace's thin lips curled up in a smug smile. "She's had a run-in with most everyone here at some point or another."

"Even you?" Coleen asked, and Shannon smiled at her friend for her perfect timing.

Grace vehemently shook her head. "No, but I'm about the only one."

Shannon pulled a business card from her tote bag and handed it to Lilly. "Please give me a call if you think of anything that could help."

Shannon stepped to the side and waited for Coleen to join her.

"That didn't go well, did it?" Coleen asked.

"Depends on how you look at it. We *are* narrowing down our suspect list—only Peter Needlemeyer and Cassandra Presley are left. We may be closing in on the real culprit."

Coleen scratched her head. "So what now?"

Shannon scanned the crowd. "Cassandra's not in here, so our best bet is to head over to the Purls' table and talk to Betty to see if Peter's alibi story panned out with Tom."

When they arrived at the table, Betty and Melanie were helping customers select sweaters. Betty looked up, and Shannon caught her attention.

Betty bagged a large sweater and handed it to the customer. Then she turned to Shannon and smiled. "At this rate, we'll be out of sweaters by the end of the day."

Shannon gave Betty a thumbs-up signal. "Then you've done a fabulous job selling them."

"The sweaters sell themselves. All we have to do is take the money." The laugh lines around Betty's eyes crinkled from her smile.

"I'm sorry I haven't been much help with that," Shannon said.

"You are helping—Kate. She needs you more than we do at the moment."

"I just want you to know I'd be here with you if I could."

"We all know that." Betty glanced at the customers. "Yikes, the line is getting long again. I really need to get back."

"Before you go, I wanted to know if you had a chance to ask Tom if he remembered Peter Needlemeyer hanging around the lobby when Millicent was killed."

"Oh, yes, I did ask him. This probably isn't what you want to hear, but Tom remembers him quite well. He said the guy was so loud and offensive that he chased away a bunch of our guests."

Shannon sighed out her frustration. "He was my top suspect."

Betty continued, "Tom also told me that Peter left the lobby for a while and then came back."

Coleen clutched Shannon's arm and asked, "Was he gone long enough to travel to Millicent's house and back?"

Betty nodded. "Tom couldn't be positive of how long he was gone, but he thinks it was about an hour."

Coleen's eyes widened. "So Peter lied to you, Shannon!"

"He certainly didn't tell me the whole truth."

"Doesn't much matter which one it is," Betty said. "Either way, he's still a viable suspect—right?"

"That he is." Shannon gave Betty a quick hug. "He's such a creepy man, and he had it in for Millicent. It's easy to picture him as her murderer. Now all I need to do is prove it."

Coleen tapped her watch. "Not now you don't. We need to get you home and cleaned up for your big date."

* * *

Shannon stood before the full-length mirror in her bedroom and studied her reflection. She'd slipped into a black sheath dress with a scooped neckline and had added a simple strand of pearls. She eyed her reflection as she nervously smoothed the straight skirt. She hadn't worn the sleek dress since Coleen's twenty-fifth wedding anniversary celebration two years ago.

"Knock, knock," Coleen said from the doorway. "Can I come in?"

"Yes, of course." Shannon turned and smiled at her friend.

Coleen whistled as she crossed the room. "You look stunning."

"Thank you. I'm shocked that the dress still fits." Shannon twirled her hair into a bun and secured it with combs. "Do you think wearing my hair up is too formal?"

"Absolutely not. Michael won't be able to take his eyes off you."

A wave of anxiety flashed through Shannon, and she sighed. "I'm not sure I'm ready for this."

"Those are pre-date jitters talking. It's normal to feel

that way." Coleen laughed. "Not that I can remember what pre-date jitters feel like."

Shannon searched Coleen's eyes. "You think that's all it is?"

"I do."

Shannon dropped her ice-cold hands to her lap and clutched them together. "I'm not sure I can do this, Coleen."

Coleen waved a hand in the air. "Nonsense. You're the strongest woman I know. Once Michael picks you up and you're on your way to Portland, you'll be fine."

Will I be fine, or will I make a complete fool of myself?

The doorbell rang, and Shannon jumped. "Oh my goodness, he's here."

"I'll go let him in."

After a quick spritz of perfume and a tuck of a stray strand into her hairclip, Shannon nodded at her reflection in the mirror. She picked up her small black clutch, slipped her cellphone inside, and grabbed a silky wrap. Telling herself that everything would go smoothly, and she and Michael were going to have a lovely evening, she stepped into the hallway.

As she approached the banister, she heard Coleen chatting with him in the foyer. Hearing his voice sent a wave of butterflies fluttering in her stomach.

"You can do this," she whispered to herself as she started down the stairs.

She'd only taken a few steps when Michael looked up, and their gazes met. His eyes widened in appreciation, and she felt a blush creep up her neck. To keep her frazzled nerves from causing a fall, she slid her hand lightly over the wooden banister as she descended.

He met her at the foot of the stairs. "You look amazing."

"Thank you." She took in his perfectly tailored suit and crisp white shirt. "You don't look so bad yourself."

His lips tipped in a genuine smile, and she felt herself start to relax.

"When can I expect you two kids home?" Coleen asked with a twinkle in her eye.

"It's hard to say. Don't wait up." He winked and turned to Shannon. "Are you ready to go?"

"Absolutely."

As Shannon stepped to the door, she thought she saw his hand tremble. Maybe he was nervous too. It *had* been ten years since his wife died. It was possible he hadn't dated in a very long time either.

He took her arm as she descended the stone steps leading to the drive, and she appreciated the support for her jittery legs. A cool breeze drifted off the ocean, causing her to tug her wrap tighter to her body.

"I see you decided against renting the convertible," she teased. "What if I'd showed up smelling like a fruity poodle, as you say?"

"I took you at your word. But a convertible might've been a good idea after all." Michael opened the passenger door of his Lexus and stood back. "Looks like we'll have perfect weather for the drive."

"I love this time of year." Shannon smiled up at him.

He flashed a heart-tripping smile and offered his hand. She laid her fingers in his and slid into his sedan. She settled on the seat, the scent of sandalwood clinging to leather. Michael got in and fired up the car. As he started off, Shannon noticed Coleen watching from the door. She waved to her friend, her pulse thrumming.

"How long is Coleen staying?" Michael clicked on the blinker.

"You know," Shannon said with surprise, "we've been so busy, we haven't talked about it. If I had my way, she'd never go back to Scotland."

"Good friends like Coleen are hard to find," he said wistfully as he turned onto the narrow country road.

"You and Grayson seem to be pretty good friends," she mused. "Though I can't imagine he's easy to get along with much of the time."

He chuckled. "Grayson's a good man, and we share the love of police business. We're friends, but not great friends."

"Well, you must have at least one good friend."

Michael arched a brow. "You make me sound unlikeable."

She shot up a hand. "No, no. That's not what I meant."

"I know. I was teasing you."

"Ah, so that's how it is." She grinned and turned to look out the window at the tall pines as they rushed past.

Michael merged onto the scenic highway, and their car climbed into the mountain range. "You'll meet my closest friend tonight," he said. "My business partner, William McCrary, and I go way back. We both enlisted in the Army on our eighteenth birthdays."

"Eighteen? That's so young." Shannon shuddered. "I can't imagine my son in the Army at this age."

Michael shrugged. "We were young, but we grew up fast under the Army's discipline."

"Your parents must not have liked it though."

"Times were different back then. Kids weren't as spoiled as they are today."

She swiveled. "Are you saying my kids are spoiled?"

"Not at all," he said quickly. "I was speaking more in general terms." He met her gaze and held it for a moment. "We seem to be getting off on the wrong foot tonight."

"I'm sorry." She clutched her hands together. "The truth is ... I'm nervous."

"So it's not just me?" He let out a sigh. "I don't do this often, you know."

"I don't either." She paused. "Never, in fact."

He nodded as if she'd said something wise. "Let's agree to relax and enjoy the night. No pressure. No expectations. Fair enough?"

"That sounds fantastic," she answered and felt her anxiety melt away.

Suddenly, Michael tensed. He sat up straighter and alternated his focus between the side and rearview mirrors.

Concerned, Shannon asked, "What's wrong?"

"The SUV behind us has been riding my bumper since we left town." Michael checked the rearview mirror again. His jaw tightened as did his fingers on the steering wheel.

Shannon's gaze flew to Michael's. "It could be someone in a hurry who wants to pass."

"There was a passing lane on this hill, and he didn't take it."

She glanced out the back window at the white SUV riding too close for safety. The vehicle didn't have an Oregon license plate, and she didn't recognize the state. The tinted glass kept her from making out the driver's details. "Do you think he's following us?"

"It appears that way." He glanced in his rearview mirror again. "And if I had to guess, I'd say it has something to do with your inquiries into Millicent's death."

Shannon spun toward Michael, fear racing down her back.

"The note," she whispered.

"What note?"

"A threat left on my windshield last night. It told me to back off the investigation or pay the price. What if this is the same person trying to make good on the threat?"

— 15 —

"Someone threatened you?" Michael demanded. "Why didn't you tell me?"

"It wasn't a big deal—just a little note on my windshield."

"Couple that with the man lurking outside your house, and it *is* a big deal." He glanced in his mirror.

Shannon looked out the rear window again. The SUV showed no sign of backing off. If anything, it had inched even closer, the roar of its powerful engine sounding through their vehicle. Holding her breath, she braced herself for the SUV to ram into the back of Michael's sedan.

"There's a turnout ahead." Michael pointed up the hill where the road widened for a scenic outlook. "I'll slow and pull over to give him once last chance to pass."

"And if he doesn't pass?"

"We'll deal with that when it happens," he answered in his usual calm manner.

Though still uneasy about the situation, Shannon knew if anyone could keep them safe, Michael could.

"Here we go," he said as he lifted his foot from the gas pedal. As his car slowed, he eased it into the turnout lane.

Shannon peered through the back window. The SUV remained in the main lane and zoomed up next to them.

"Oh no, I think he's going to sideswipe us!" Shannon

tried to get a good look at the driver, but the tinted glass blocked most everything. All she could make out was an outline confirming the driver was a large man.

"It's going to be OK." Michael tipped his head toward the side of the road. "We're protected by guardrails."

Protected or not, as the driver gunned his engine, Shannon's heart pounded hard, and nausea threatened her stomach. She clutched the door handle and braced herself for impact.

Surprisingly, it never came.

The SUV suddenly shot forward. With the roar of the engine, he passed them and zoomed up the hill.

"There's a notepad and pen in the console." Michael didn't take his eyes off the road. "Can you write down the license plate number?"

With trembling hands, she retrieved the items, and as Michael called out the numbers, she jotted them down.

At the top of the hill, he pulled the car onto the turnout and stopped. Then he held out his hand for the notepad. He grabbed his phone from a dash holder and dialed. "Let's see if we can learn our mystery driver's identity."

"You can do that?" she asked, amazed by his unruffled demeanor.

He nodded and held up a finger.

"It's Michael," he said into his phone. "I need an Arizona plate run immediately." He repeated the numbers using words for the letters. "I'll wait." He glanced at Shannon. "This should only take a few seconds."

"I never imagined you'd have access to DMV records."

He smiled, but it was forced. "It pays to have friends in the right places." He tucked the phone under his ear. "OK, go ahead." He scribbled something on his notepad. "Text me when you've located the agreement."

He tossed the notepad into the holder. "It's a rental car. My associates are trying to obtain a copy of the rental agreement to determine the driver's identity."

"Will they be able to do that?"

He shifted into gear. "The rental company isn't supposed to give out personal information without a warrant, but my people are pros."

Shannon couldn't think of anything to say in response. She didn't know the Michael who had access to government records and worked with people who wormed information from others. Sure, she'd gotten glimpses of the hardnosed investigator when he'd come to her rescue, but she hadn't taken the time to think about his profession and what he must do on a daily basis.

"I'm sorry this happened tonight of all nights," he said as he merged into the light traffic. "But why don't you bring me up to speed on what you've learned about Millicent's murder? That way, if the man *was* tailing us as a result of your sleuthing activities, we're better prepared to deal with him, should our paths cross again." He offered her a comforting look.

She didn't feel the least bit comforted. "When you say 'deal with it,' do you mean this man could be waiting for us up ahead?"

"It's possible."

My first date in eons ... and it's interrupted by a murderer. "What do you want to know?" she asked.

"Tell me more about your suspects."

Shannon filled him in on Peter and Cassandra and why she still felt they were likely suspects.

Michael frowned. "You say Cassandra's a top suspect, but is that all you've got on her?"

At his incredulous tone, a flicker of irritation lit inside, but Shannon quickly squashed it. They were on a date, and she wasn't about to get into an argument. "She doesn't have an alibi, and she's tall and right-handed, fitting the medical examiner's criteria for the killer. Plus, the bite mark on her arm could be from Scarlet, and the drops of blood found near the crate in Millicent's den might belong to Cassandra."

"If so, Grayson can test the blood. Have you told him?" Michael asked.

"Yes, but he hasn't said anything to me about the results."

"He probably won't. He doesn't like you interfering in his investigations. I'll ask him about it."

She shot Michael a surprised look. "I'm not trying to interfere. My goal is to help."

"I understand. But if I were him, I'd probably be irritated with you too."

Her jaw dropped open. "How can you say that?"

"Don't misunderstand. I'm not saying I *am* irritated with you. Quite the contrary." He sent a dazzling smile her way.

She stared at him, fully aware that she should be annoyed, or at the very least look away. But he had the most beguiling smile ...

Michael spoke again, snapping her out of her trance. "That said, if I were the officer in charge of this case, I'd resent the interference of an amateur."

She raised her chin. "Even if I solved the crime?"

"Maybe more so if you kept solving crimes before me and ruining my street credibility," he teased good-naturedly.

"I guess I never stopped to think about it that way. I'm certainly not trying to taint Grayson's reputation." She considered her actions from Grayson's point of view. "I know he's a good man."

Michael waited, an amused expression on his face. "But?"

"But what? I promised Kate I'd help her, and I'm getting close to unraveling this mess. I can't back off now."

He laughed, warm and hearty. "Yes, well, I assumed that would be a tall order. You're irresistibly stubborn."

His laughter was contagious, and their conversation for the rest of the ride remained easygoing. When they arrived at a historic hotel in downtown Portland, she was surprised to realize she'd forgotten all about the incident with the white SUV.

As Michael pulled up to valet parking, she peered through her window at the ornate columns and intricate moldings on the building. She'd expected Michael would host a nice dinner, but this hotel went beyond first class to world class—a class in which Shannon's humble upbringing left her feeling a little uncomfortable.

The valet opened her door, and she slid out. A chill nipped at her arms, so she shook out her wrap and started to put it on, but before she could do so, Michael took the soft fabric from her hands. He settled it over her shoulders, sending a new shiver through her as his fingertips lightly grazed her skin.

"Thank you." She smiled up at him.

He offered her his arm. "Shall we?"

Together, they entered the ostentatious lobby filled with ornate gold reliefs and colorful paintings on the ceiling. A large sign next to the polished wooden desk announced that Stone & McCrary's event was located in a ballroom on the second floor.

"My goodness, I had no idea your company was big enough to need a ballroom," Shannon said. She gazed around at the spacious lobby, inhaling the warm vanilla scent that hung in the air.

"It's a small ballroom." He put a gentle hand on her back and directed her to an elevator with glass walls.

On the ride up, she slipped off her wrap and looked over the atrium at the lush green plants, the fine furnishings, and the uniformed staff who catered to well-dressed guests. It was such a foreign world to her that she would've been quite content to stay there and watch it unfold, but when the elevator doors opened, Michael checked his watch and ushered her out into the long hallway. As they neared the ballroom entrance, a tall, thin man with a receding hairline saluted Michael.

"That's my partner, William McCrary," Michael said as they crossed the plush carpet.

When they reached William, he turned the full force of his deep brown eyes on Shannon. "I'm certain you never mentioned you'd be bringing a guest, Stone."

William's intense scrutiny set her earlier butterflies fluttering again in her stomach.

"I'd like you to meet my ... ah—" Michael fell silent for a moment. "My good friend, Shannon McClain."

Shannon didn't miss Michael's pause, nor did William, who raised a brow and offered his hand. "Hello, *good friend* Shannon."

"Is everything set?" Michael asked.

"I've got it under control." William didn't bother to look at Michael when he answered. Instead, he kept hold of Shannon's hand. "So tell me about yourself, Sha—"

"There's no time." Michael tersely cut him off and turned to Shannon. "Let's find our seats, and you can put down your wrap before the guests arrive."

William released her hand. "That's fine, run off," he said to their departing backs. "We'll have plenty of time to talk later."

Shannon felt Michael stiffen next to her, and she wondered why he'd asked her to join him if he didn't want her to talk with his partner. Had he just realized it had been a bad idea to invite her?

"We have assigned seats," Michael said, heading down a narrow aisle between rows of tables. At the front of the space, he stepped up on a platform, then pointed at a chair behind a long table. "That's you."

Shannon's eyes widened. *We're sitting on the dais?* She hadn't prepared herself for people gawking at her and wondering about their relationship as she ate.

"We should get back to the door and greet the guests." Michael took her wrap and draped it over her chair.

There's a receiving line too? Shannon looked longingly at her chair. Would it be rude of her to remain here instead? Of course it would, and she wasn't rude. She might be nervous, but she hadn't been raised without social graces.

"You're freaked out by all of this, aren't you?" Michael watched her with intense eyes. "I should never have asked you to such a public event for our first date." He stepped closer. "I'm sorry. Do you want me to take you home?"

She gave herself a mental shake and smiled. "I'm not freaked out. I'm quite enjoying myself, actually. And I won't melt under a little scrutiny. I'm a hearty Scottish lass, re-member?"

He let out a relieved breath, and they started for the door. For the next hour, she stood smiling and nodding as Michael introduced her as his "friend." She understood his reluctance to call her his date in front of his employees, and she didn't mind a bit. She knew the truth—he'd said so himself. He considered the evening a date, and she couldn't deny that she was happy by the confirmation—slightly giddy over it, in fact.

After Michael welcomed the last person in line, he turned to her. "You've been a real trooper. Thanks."

"You're welcome. Now could I be wimpy for a moment and ask if we could take a quick break?" She flashed a smile. "Maybe get some fresh air?"

"There's a balcony a few doors down with a great view of the river. Come with me."

Unaccustomed to standing in dress shoes for long peri-ods of time, Shannon's feet ached as they walked down the hallway. But the moment she caught sight of the sun setting over the Willamette River, she forgot all about the pain and hurried to the stone balusters at the edge of the balcony. "It's gorgeous!" she cried out.

"I was thinking the very same thing," he said.

At the softness in his tone, she turned and caught him watching her, admiration gleaming in his eyes. A wave of heat washed up her face, and she knew she was coloring as bright as the setting sun. Embarrassed, she looked away.

As she did, a flash of movement by the entrance caught her eye. Before she could even process it, a burly man bolted from the shadows, wielding a large knife in his hand.

Running full force toward her, he roared like a lion and raised his knife overhead.

As she watched him approach, time seemed to stop, and everything moved in slow motion. Step after step, he came closer—his eyes hot and mean, his expression ugly. The large knife glinted in the overhead light as his hand shook with rage.

She heard Michael shout—"No!"

Terror lit her heart as she searched for a way out, but she was trapped. She retreated until her back connected with the cool stone railing, pinning her in front of the crazed man.

— 16 —

"Stop, Gillespie!" Michael yelled as he threw himself in front of Shannon.

Caught off guard, the crazed man's steps faltered.

"Give it up," Michael warned as he eased toward his husky assailant.

"Never," Gillespie answered. "Not as long as you're still breathing." His arm came down with a mighty plunge.

Michael's hand shot out and deflected Gillespie's arm with an upward blow to his wrist.

With rage burning brighter, Gillespie snarled and plunged the knife down again. Michael sidestepped, the blade barely missing his arm.

Gillespie couldn't stop his forward motion. He slammed into the concrete wall near Shannon and ricocheted off. Spinning like a windmill, his arms flailed in the air to regain his balance. His knife-wielding hand came down, and the butt of the knife slammed into Shannon's head.

A bolt of pain sliced through her skull. The knife shot free and flew through the air before clattering to the floor.

"Oh!" she cried out as she lost her footing. She thrust out a hand and grabbed the railing. The rough concrete bit into her skin, but she held on and remained upright.

Gillespie lost his balance and plummeted to the floor.

In a flash, Michael dropped onto Gillespie and slammed his knee in the man's back.

"It's over, Gillespie." Michael wrenched his attacker's arms behind his back.

"You know this man?" Shannon finally recovered enough to speak.

"We caught his wife embezzling from her company."

"Says you," Gillespie spit out and squirmed again. "You set her up."

Michael jerked Gillespie's arms higher until he stopped struggling. "The judge and jury who convicted her didn't see it your way." Michael searched Shannon's face. "I'm so sorry. Are you all right?"

"I'm fine," she answered, but her trembling voice gave away her apprehension over nearly losing her life.

Clenching his jaw, Michael dug his cellphone from his jacket pocket with his free hand. He thumbed the screen and lifted the phone to his ear. "I need you on the balcony *now*." He stowed his phone. "William will be here soon. Are you sure you're all right? You look a little pale."

"I'm OK." She rested her hand on the wall to steady herself, but the concrete burn left her hand hot with pain, so she let go.

"There are chairs by the door. Why don't you sit down?"

Thankful for his suggestion, she crossed the space on wobbly legs and dropped onto an outdoor sofa. Relief flooded her body, and she was suddenly thankful she'd sat. Her head throbbed, and her hands burned. But she was alive—thanks to Michael, who was still watching her, his expression filled with concern.

Footsteps pounded down the hall, and William burst

into the space. With an assessing glance, he dropped to the floor and took over for Michael. "What happened?"

"Gillespie attacked me." Michael stretched his arms and back. "You remember him, right?"

William nodded. "Did you call the police?"

"Not yet," Michael said. "I'll call now that you're here."

He took out his cellphone and dialed. Wedging his phone between his shoulder and ear, he made his way to Shannon. "You're bleeding. Here, let me see."

She turned her head to the side, giving him access. He gently probed, hitting a tender area.

"Ouch," she said involuntarily.

"Sorry. There's not a lot of blood, but I'll request an ambulance too."

She frowned. "No ambulance. It's a little bump. I'm fine."

"I insist. Head injuries are nothing to take lightly."

Shannon wanted to argue about the ambulance, but she didn't have the strength. Feeling safe in his very capable hands, she closed her eyes and rested her head on the back of the sofa.

When the EMT arrived, Michael gave her a rundown of Shannon's injuries.

The medic knelt down next to Shannon. "Did you lose consciousness?"

"No."

The medic probed the wound just like Michael had, but when pain made Shannon draw in a sharp breath, she didn't apologize or stop probing.

The medic sat back on her heels. "Any nausea or vomiting?"

Shannon shook her head.

"It looks minor, but a blow to the head can cause serious problems. You'll need to be checked out in the ER."

"That's not necessary," Shannon insisted, imbuing her voice with the strength she didn't feel. "It's just a scratch."

"Don't argue." Michael's tone was harsher than she'd ever heard, drawing her head up.

She cringed at the increased pain the movement caused. "I'll have it checked out when we get back to Apple Grove."

"Can you excuse us a minute?" Michael asked the EMT.

She raised her brows and stepped away.

Michael sat next to Shannon. He plowed his hands into his hair and gazed at her until she wanted to squirm. "I get that you don't want to go to the hospital, but Gillespie could have seriously hurt you. I'd like confirmation that he didn't. They'll take a simple CT scan, and then we can go."

"Honestly, Michael, I'm fine. We can go back to Apple Grove, and I'll see a doctor at the urgent care clinic there."

He appraised her silently for a moment. "How about we compromise? I'll take you to an urgent care clinic before we leave Portland. That way, if they recommend a hospital visit, we'll be near a hospital instead of on a long drive home."

She was certain Gillespie hadn't hit her hard enough to need a visit, but she knew he wouldn't give up. "It's a deal."

"Good. I'll give my statement to the police and tell William where we're going. Then we'll get out of here." He stood.

"Wait. What about the dinner and the awards? You should be here for that."

"William can take care of it." He spun on his heel and walked away.

Sighing at the debacle their date had become, Shannon carefully leaned her head back and closed her eyes until it was time to go. Michael returned and helped her to his car, which was waiting at the curb for them.

Once on the road, she gave him a weak smile. "I'm sorry I ruined your evening."

"You didn't ruin anything." He tightened his hands around the wheel and glanced at her. His usually vibrant eyes held anguish. "I'll get to the clinic as fast as I can."

"Try not to break any traffic laws," she said, trying to keep her tone light. "We've already had to involve the police and an ambulance on our first date. I'd hate for the night to end with you being thrown in jail."

*　*　*

Hours later, Shannon leaned against the soft layer of silk pillows propped against her headboard. With an ice pack on her head, she stared at the lacy canopy draping her teak four-poster bed. She felt Coleen's watchful eyes peering at her from the other side of the room. Coleen had mothered her from the moment she'd stepped in the door, and she was starting to feel like a bug under a microscope. After Michael's thorough care—which had included a quick doctor's visit—she could hardly endure the same intensity from her dear friend.

"Would you stop looking at me like that?" Shannon said. "You'd think I was at death's door."

Coleen crossed the room and glared down on Shannon. "I'd leave you alone if I didn't know you're too stubborn to let anyone know when you need help."

"Trust me, if the urgent care doctor had told me to go to the hospital, I would have."

Coleen settled on the edge of the bed. "Michael seemed to think you should have gone to the hospital anyway."

"Michael isn't a doctor, and he's being overprotective."

"He is, isn't he?" Coleen grinned and scooted closer. "Rather romantic, isn't it?"

Shannon hadn't thought of his behavior as "romantic," but if she stretched her imagination, she supposed she could classify his overly attentive actions as being so.

Coleen tilted her head and appraised Shannon. "Now tell me all about the date before the deranged man attacked you."

"There's nothing to tell." Shannon sighed. "It wasn't much of a date, considering everything that happened."

"Well, don't fret. Michael will ask you out again, and you can have a second go at it." Coleen squeezed Shannon's hand. "You do want him to ask again—don't you?"

Shannon smiled. "Very much."

"Brilliant!" Coleen clapped her hands together, her eyes gleaming. "I'm so happy for you."

A spark of happiness lit in Shannon's heart as well. "Before you start planning our wedding, let's wait and see if he'll ask me out again. He may decide we're too volatile of a combination."

"Oh, he'll ask."

Shannon frowned. "I don't know. He was strangely quiet on the way home."

"He probably thought you needed to rest."

"Could be—and he's right." Shannon yawned on cue. "As much as I want to stay up and talk with you, I need to get a good night's sleep. I've got a lot to do tomorrow."

Coleen clucked her tongue. "If you mean making more inquiries into Millicent's death, I think you should take the day off. Kate will surely understand."

"I can't," Shannon said forcefully to preempt additional arguments. "It's the last day of the dog show, and the owners will all be leaving. If I don't make any more headway tomorrow, I fear that will be the end of my investigation. I will have been of no help to Kate whatsoever."

"Still, I think you should wait and see how you feel in the morning." Coleen stood and adjusted Shannon's covers. "A knock to the head is nothing to play around with."

Shannon's cellphone rang from the nightstand, eliciting a scowl from Coleen. "Who would be calling you this late at night?" she asked.

Shannon grabbed the phone and spotted her mother's icon.

"It's Beth." Shannon answered the call. "Hello."

"I'm sorry for calling you so late," Beth said. "But I heard your name on the news and wanted to see if everything was all right."

"I was on the news?" Shannon glanced at Coleen, who widened her eyes with surprise.

"There was a story about the attack at the hotel. The reporter said they had the attacker in custody, but the report didn't specify who had the minor injuries."

"That would be me." Shannon said. "But I'm OK, and so is Michael. I just bumped my head."

Beth continued, "They didn't say why it happened. I thought if it was connected to the recent murder in Apple Grove that it might help me to convince you to let the chief handle the investigating for awhile. I'm worried about you." Her words rushed out in a torrent.

"There's no need to worry. The attack had nothing to do with Millicent Downing's death. The man was trying to get back at Michael for putting his wife in prison. I was just in the wrong place at the wrong time."

Beth let out a whoosh of air. "I'm so glad to hear that—well, you know what I mean."

Shannon chuckled. "I do."

"Will I see you tomorrow at the show, or are you planning to take the day off to recover?"

"I'll be there."

"Then I'll say goodbye for now."

"Goodnight. Thanks for calling." Shannon settled her phone on the nightstand.

"She didn't try to talk you out of going tomorrow?" Coleen asked with reproach as she adjusted Shannon's covers again.

Shannon started to shake her head, but pain stopped her. "Surprisingly, no."

"I suppose she feels she has no right to interfere." Coleen reached for the lamp switch. "I'm not such a pushover. Get a good night's sleep, and we'll talk more in the morning about why you should stay home."

Shannon simply smiled. No matter how she felt in the morning, she planned to be at the show. Kate needed her help, and a little bump on the head wasn't going to prevent her from doing all she could to identify Millicent's true killer.

— 17 —

Running late the next morning, Shannon rummaged through her medicine cabinet for aspirin and swallowed two tablets. With her head throbbing and her hands burning, she wanted nothing more than to drop back into bed and pull the covers up to her chin, but she couldn't miss the last day of the dog show—her final chance to talk to the dog owners while they were all in town.

She checked her face in the mirror and groaned at her tired and battered reflection. She hadn't slept well, and even a long soak in the lavender-infused tub hadn't eased her exhaustion or soreness.

With a sigh, she grabbed a sweater and headed downstairs. As she neared the kitchen, she heard Coleen chatting with Deborah, the two of them laughing together. Despite the lecture she knew was coming from Coleen, the heavenly scent of freshly brewed coffee pulled Shannon toward the kitchen.

When she entered the room, Coleen and Deborah stopped talking and looked at her. Shannon ignored their stares and grabbed a cup of coffee. Her back to the women, she said, "You can both stop looking at me. I'm fine and I'll be heading into town shortly." She turned and faced Coleen. "No arguments."

Coleen crossed her arms. "Far be it from me, your dearest friend in the entire world, to tell you that you look like death warmed over, and the last place you need to be is in a busy park surrounded by people—at least one of whom may prefer that you were dead."

"That's quite a speech." Shannon took a long sip of her coffee.

Coleen cleared her throat disapprovingly. "I see you're not going to listen to reason."

"No."

"Fine. I'm coming with you."

Shannon smiled. "I wouldn't have it any other way."

"I've cooked a batch of scrambled eggs." Deborah stepped in as if they needed a peacemaker. "The protein will do you good. Can I fix you a plate?"

The throbbing pain left Shannon with little appetite, but she had less of an appetite for arguing with her wonderful housekeeper about the importance of breakfast. "That would be great."

Shannon took the chair across the table from Coleen, who watched her with narrowed eyes. "What?"

"You agree with Deborah without a fuss but argue with me?"

"Offer me something reasonable like Deborah's fluffy eggs," Shannon said with a smile, "and I'll say yes to you too."

"Hmm." Coleen took a sip of her tea and regarded Shannon over the rim of the cup. "So what's on the agenda this morning?"

"My first priority is to show the pictures from Millicent's house to Kate one last time. I can't shake the feeling that we're missing something there."

"Maybe if I take a look at them again, I'll see something you've missed," Coleen offered.

"Good idea. I'll go grab them from the study." Shannon started to rise.

Coleen held out her hand. "Sit. I'll get the pictures if you tell me where to find them."

"In the tote bag hanging on the back of my desk chair."

Humming, Coleen sauntered out of the room, her flip-flops snapping loudly with each step.

Deborah set a plate of eggs and thick wheat toast in front of Shannon. "Let me know if you want seconds."

"Thanks." Smelling the food made Shannon suddenly very hungry, and she wolfed down the eggs as if she hadn't eaten in a week. When she finished, she sat back and stretched her sore muscles. Full and content, she felt ready to take on the dog-show world.

*   *   *

With pictures of Millicent's house tucked safely inside her bag, Shannon said goodbye to Coleen at the Purls' charity booth and hurried down the sidewalk in search of Kate. Betty had had to remain at the inn to check out departing guests, so Coleen had volunteered to help Joyce set up for the morning.

"Shannon?" Michael's unmistakable voice came from behind.

She smiled and turned. "Just the man I was hoping to see today."

As he moved closer, she inhaled the spicy scent of his cologne. His face spoke of a sleepless night, and Shannon wondered if he'd lain awake thinking about Gillespie's attack.

He didn't return her smile. Instead he fixed a firm gaze on her. "I didn't expect to see you here today."

She felt exposed under his scrutiny. "I have things to do."

"But you should be resting."

"I'll rest later," she snapped and instantly regretted it. "I'm sorry. That was so cranky. Coleen's been watching me like a hawk since you left last night, and I'm starting to feel claustrophobic from all the fuss."

Still no sign of a smile on his lips. "I'm sure she means well."

"I know, and I love her for it." Shannon answered. "Are you here for a particular reason today, or did you come as a spectator?" She rubbed her temples. "That didn't come out quite right either."

Anguish filled his eyes. "I'm so sorry that you got hurt last night."

A lump swelled in her throat, but she swallowed it before he could see how shaken the attack had left her. "It's not your fault that Gillespie attacked me."

He took a deep, pained breath and looked away.

"You're blaming yourself." She took a step closer and placed her hand on his arm. "You shouldn't."

He shrugged, still avoiding her gaze. "Is there anything I can do to help you today so you can get some rest?"

"You could tell me if you've seen Kate."

"I haven't." He looked down at her hand on his arm.

Feeling self-conscious, she pulled it away. "I guess I'll go see if she's at her shop. I'll talk to you later?" She forced out a smile.

He nodded, but his lips remained in a tight, thin line. *OK then.*

She walked down the sidewalk and soon found Kate balancing a large cardboard box while trying to lock the door to her shop. Wisps of hair that had escaped from her ponytail floated in the breeze, and as she reached up to push them out of her face, she dropped her keys.

"Let me help you," Shannon called out.

Kate spun, frowning when she caught sight of Shannon. "I'm surprised to see you here today. Are you sure you're up to all of this?"

"Et tu, Brute?" Shannon mumbled, not at all surprised Kate had heard about the attack.

"What?"

"Nothing." Shannon took the box, her raw hands aching from the weight. "Would you have time to look at the photos of Millicent's house one more time?"

"I suppose, but if I have to look at them again, I want to do so over a cup of coffee." Kate picked up her keys and locked the door.

"I'll make your favorite drink for you. Come with me."

They set off together down the sidewalk devoid of dogs or people. The show didn't start until noon, and Shannon figured the owners were sleeping in. She shifted the box to her hip to ease the strain on her hands.

"Are you sure you're all right? I can take the box if it's too heavy," Kate offered.

"I've got it," Shannon said, lest Kate join everyone else in thinking she should be resting at home.

"So?" Kate asked.

Shannon felt Kate's expectant stare upon her. "So what?"

"Aside from the terrifying knife attack, how was the date?"

After her recent exchange with Michael, Shannon wasn't sure how to respond. But she decided she could probably use a little advice, and as a single female, Kate would be the perfect person to dispense it. "Have you ever gone out with a guy, thought the date went well—factoring out any deranged man who may have tried to stab you with a knife—"

Kate snorted. "Goes without saying."

"—and then the next day, your date acts kind of stand-offish?"

"Hmm. I usually don't see the guy the next day, but I've had dates that I thought went well, but he never called me again." Kate stopped in front of the craft market. "Is that what's happening with Michael?"

Shannon handed the box to Kate so she could dig out her keys. "Yes. Up until 'the incident' last night, we were having a good time. I really felt like we'd gotten past that awkward stage, you know?"

Kate nodded. "When it feels like you're dancing on glass."

"Exactly." Shannon inserted her key in the lock. "But I ran in to him today, and it feels like we're back to that weird state where everything we say to each other is wrong and uncomfortable."

"Could it have anything to do with the attack? I mean, you know what happened to his wife ..."

Shannon nodded. "I suspect it does. He acted like he felt guilty that I got hurt." She pushed open the door and stood back. "But I've tried to make it crystal clear that I don't blame him for what happened."

Kate stepped inside and set the box on the floor. "I wish I knew the answer for you. Men are a tough breed to figure out most of the time."

"Truer words were never spoken," Shannon said and decided to drop the subject until after she'd had a chance to think about it more. "What can I get you to drink?"

Kate crossed the room. "I could use something really sugary this morning."

Shannon stepped behind the bar and appraised her friend. "Are you holding up OK?"

"Honestly?" Kate climbed onto a stool. "No. I'm worried about what will happen to me if we don't find the killer today before everyone leaves. I'm sorry. I know I've been nothing but self-absorbed lately, and you've got a lot on your plate already. I'm just terrified of going to jail for a crime I didn't commit."

"We can still get to the bottom of this mess today, and we'll start with the pictures." Shannon set her bag on the counter, pulled out the pictures, and set them in front of Kate. "Look over these again while I make your latte."

Kate sighed. "We've been through these so many times. What can we possibly hope to find?"

"I don't know. Anything that's out of place." Shannon moved to the dispensers and pumped thick caramel syrup into a paper cup. "Why don't you focus today on the dog-related stuff in the room since I don't know much about dogs?"

Kate started flipping through the pictures. She turned them over quickly. *Too quickly to be studying them thoroughly.* Shannon bit her tongue as she added coffee that Essie had brewed earlier. It blended with the syrup, turning the liquid a rich caramel color.

"Here you go." Shannon set Kate's drink on the counter and took the photos from her. She separated the first picture from the others and pointed at a black plastic case sitting on a corner table in the photo. "Do you know what this is?"

Kate swirled her drink as she stared at the picture. "The case holds a professional clipper."

"I thought you groomed Scarlet now."

"I do, but Millicent used to groom her exclusively, and she did touch-ups between visits with me." Kate sipped her latte and moaned with pleasure. "Thanks. I really needed this sugar."

Shannon smiled at her friend before returning her focus to the photo. Bottles of shampoo and other products sat next to the case. "Isn't it a little odd that Millicent kept grooming supplies in her den?"

"Odd for you and me maybe, but Millicent lived for Scarlet. She didn't have any friends who'd come to visit, so it didn't matter where she kept the dog items."

Shannon flipped through the remaining photographs and then dropped them onto the counter. "I guess that's it then. I don't see anything to help us in these pictures."

Kate stood. "I should get going anyway. I need to replenish the items at my booth before the crowd descends on us."

"Have your sales been good?" Shannon snapped a lid on Kate's drink.

"Exceptional. I've nearly depleted my inventory of dog

toys. I had to come in early this morning to place an order with my supplier."

Dog toys? Shannon picked up the stack of photos and flipped through them again. "Strange, there aren't many toys in these pictures."

"There shouldn't be *any* toys. Millicent said Scarlet was a working dog, and she got all the stimulation she needed in her training."

"Really? I'm sure I saw *a* toy." Shannon flipped through the photos until she spotted a purple ball lying on the floor. She handed the photo to Kate. "There's a ball by the crate."

"That's a treat ball." Kate paused. "But this is the last thing Millicent would ever give Scarlet."

"Are you sure?" Shannon asked, feeling the excitement of a lead building inside. "And what exactly is a treat ball?"

"The ball holds food. The dog chews on the ball to release the treats through the open sides. Owners often use them to keep dogs busy while they're crated. Millicent thought dogs should earn their treats through hard work; she'd never let Scarlet have a treat ball."

"But our killer might," Shannon said slowly as her theory took hold. "I bet he left it. Perhaps he arrived intending to kidnap Scarlet—not to kill Millicent. He wanted to keep Scarlet busy in the crate to keep her from barking and warning the neighbors. So he brought along a treat ball."

"Only one problem," Kate interrupted. "Why did he leave it behind?"

"If Millicent startled him and he killed her, he might've been too flustered to remember the ball. He probably grabbed Scarlet and fled."

"Makes sense."

Shannon visualized the killer fleeing with the yipping Scarlet and traveling to one of the motor homes or trailers.

"Oh, oh, oh," Shannon said as an idea popped into her mind. "It also makes sense that if the killer is still holding Scarlet captive here, he'd want to replace the missing ball to keep her busy. *And* as the only supplier of dog toys in town, he'd have to buy it from you!"

"I have sold a few of them this weekend." Kate's face lit with excitement. "Let's go to my booth and check my sales records."

"Really? You'd have the names of the people who bought treat balls in the last few days?"

Kate nodded enthusiastically. "I've been diligent at getting buyers to sign up for my dog care newsletter. I don't remember anyone saying no. I should be able to cross-reference the receipts with the list."

"But would the killer give you his real name?"

"If it was someone I'd met this weekend or knew from a dog show, they'd have to use their real name."

"Of course!" Shannon grabbed Kate's hand and pulled her toward the door. "Let's go."

— 18 —

Nearly out of breath from running, Shannon and Kate arrived at the Ultimutt Grooming booth in record time. Kate quickly slipped behind the booth and set her tote bag on the table. Shannon settled on a cold, metal folding chair and tapped her foot impatiently.

Kate retrieved a large box from under the skirted table and pulled out a thick stack of handwritten receipts. She handed half the pile to Shannon. "Too bad I don't own one of those fancy computer systems to keep track of sales."

"Look on the bright side." Shannon turned over the first receipt. "Once we finish going through these piles, we may finally know the name of Millicent's killer."

They eagerly dug into the receipts. After an hour of being hunched over in her chair, Shannon stood to get the blood flowing through her body again, her back still aching from the previous night's altercation. She lifted her arms over her shoulders and rotated her neck.

"Oh, no," Kate said, her voice filled with dread.

Shannon glanced at Kate and found her eyeing Chief Grayson across the lawn.

"He's headed this way, and he looks mad." Kate settled back in her chair and turned to Shannon. "What did you do?"

"Me? Nothing." Shannon's voice shot up, drawing his attention. She leaned closer to Kate and whispered, "Recently."

"Ladies." Grayson stopped in front of their table and planted his feet wide.

"Good morning." Shannon greeted him with a smile, hoping to diffuse his ire. "How can we help you this morning?"

"I've come to clear up a few things with Kate." He looked down at Kate. "For starters, you might have told me the *real* reason you crawled back to Millicent after she sued you."

Kate's eyebrows pinched together. "First of all, I didn't see it as crawling. When you own a business in a small town, you have to be flexible to keep your clients happy."

"I suppose with your financial issues you'd have to grovel a lot."

Shannon whipped her head toward her friend. *Kate has financial issues?*

Kate sighed, a long, drawn-out number indicative of her exhaustion. "I don't know what my finances have to do with Millicent."

Grayson eyed her. "People do desperate things for money."

"I'm not desperate, Grayson. I had a bit of a problem when the economy tanked and clients went longer between grooming appointments. Things have picked up now, and I'm doing OK. And even if I *was* desperate—which I'm not—I don't see how a dead Millicent would help my finances."

Grayson leaned in close. "You expect me to believe that you don't know about her will?"

Kate planted her arms on the lawn chair and held her ground. "What about it?"

"She left Scarlet to you."

Kate opened and closed her mouth a few times like a fish

under water before she finally found her voice. "Scarlet? To me? But why?"

"Her attorney said you were the only person she trusted to take care of her precious dog for life."

Kate sat with her jaw unhinged, still unable to form a coherent sentence.

"Even so, being saddled with a show dog wouldn't help Kate's finances," Shannon interjected.

"Oh, but that's where you're wrong." A superior look claimed Grayson's face, and Shannon braced herself for his next announcement. "If Kate kept Scarlet, her finances would improve immeasurably."

"How?" Kate challenged.

"Scarlet is contracted to star in a Doggie Delights commercial, and as Scarlet's new owner, you would receive all of the royalties."

Kate's eyes widened. "I didn't know anything about Scarlet starring in a commercial!"

"Surely Millicent told you she wanted Scarlet's hair cut short for the Doggie Delights people. They thought the viewers could relate to her better if she had shorter hair and looked more like a little fur ball."

"No!" Kate shouted. "All she said was that since Scarlet was retired, short hair would be easier to take care of."

Grayson shook his head. "This will go a lot easier for you if you just tell the truth."

Kate shot to her feet. "You have to believe me! I didn't know about any of this."

Shannon caught Grayson's gaze. "If you have evidence proving Kate knew about the commercial, I suggest you show it to us now. Otherwise, quit badgering her."

He alternated his glare between each of them. "If you won't admit the truth, I'll have to keep digging." He paused and locked eyes with Kate. "But be aware, young lady, that I always find the truth."

Kate's chin rose in defiance. "I had *nothing* to do with Millicent's death."

"Don't leave town."

Shannon leaned in close to Grayson. "What about the other suspects, like Cassandra and Peter? Have you ruled them out already?" she asked.

"Kate has the best motive for murder," Grayson said.

"So you're not going to tell me what you've learned about Cassandra or Peter?"

The chief lifted his hat then immediately resettled it. "I can tell you Peter Needlemeyer is one odd duck, and I liked him for the murder until last night. But I have unequivocal proof that he's not our killer."

Disappointment flooded Shannon. "And Cassandra?"

"I'm still waiting on the blood analysis."

"So you agree that it's *possible* Scarlet may have bitten her?"

"Anything is possible. That doesn't mean it's probable," he said. Shannon opened her mouth to ask another question, but he held up his hand. "That's all I'm saying on the subject, Shannon. I've already told you both more than I should have." His gaze darted to Kate. "If you decide you have something you want to tell me, you know where I am."

Both women watched in stunned silence as he strode away.

"Do you think he was telling the truth about Millicent's will?" Kate asked.

"Yes," Shannon answered. "I may not like the way he's conducting this investigation, but he's not a liar."

"Scarlet belongs to me now?"

"Looks like it."

Kate fell back into her chair. "Do you think he's going to arrest me for murder?"

"Not yet," Shannon said, hoping she was right. "But we don't have a second to waste. Let's get through these receipts."

"I'm on it." Kate grabbed her stack. Her hands trembled as she flipped through the papers.

Shannon had to give her friend points for holding it together as they reviewed every receipt. In the end, they set aside five receipts for customers who'd purchased treat balls in the previous three days. Shannon picked them up and looked at the names with dismay. None of them matched the names on Shannon's suspect list, and she hadn't heard their names mentioned by others as potential suspects either.

She handed the receipts to Kate. "Do you recognize any of these people?"

Kate glanced through them and set two of them aside. "I remember these two. They were tourists from Salem and happened upon the dog show. Not the most likely suspects. I think I recognize the other three from the owner registration list."

"Let's check them against your main list."

Kate grabbed her clipboard from under the table and ran her finger down the page, calling out each name as she located them. "They're not in the finals. I don't know where you're going to find them, but this might help." Kate handed the schedule to Shannon.

Shannon jotted the names in her notebook and tucked

the schedule in her bag. "I'll start at the tent and ask if anyone knows them. Hopefully they're still in town."

"Who's in town?" Coleen asked as she stepped up to the table.

"Three dog owners who bought treat balls." Shannon got up. "I'm off to the tent to see if they're still here."

"The Purls are in good shape at the booth for now, so I'll go with you." Coleen fell in step beside Shannon. "Who are you looking for?"

Shannon held out her notebook and pointed at the three names. "I'll start with the one at the top."

Coleen tapped her finger on a name. "Oliver Daniels. I introduced you to him yesterday."

Shannon thought for a moment. "The man staffing the shelter's booth?"

"Yes." Coleen's focus shifted to the far end of the path. "Is there a new reason Chief Grayson is scowling at you?"

Shannon looked in the direction Coleen indicated and spotted him standing near the grooming tent with his arms crossed.

"Unfortunately, yes." Shannon conveyed the latest accusations he'd tossed at Kate as the sound of heated voices pulled Shannon's focus away from Coleen. The racket came from behind the tall fabric walls of the Doggie Delights booth.

"Wow," Coleen said, "someone sure is mad."

Shannon nodded. "That's the company Scarlet has a contract with." She stepped toward the booth to listen to the argument.

"If she hadn't interfered," a woman shouted, "I'd have won the competition, and the commercial would be mine."

"That's not true," a male voice responded.

"It's *mine*, and I deserve it!" the woman said, then lowered her voice. "If you don't come through for me, I'll make sure you pay."

A scuffling sound followed. Hoping to see what was going on, Shannon eased alongside the booth. She heard Coleen following behind.

"How dare you touch me?" the man shouted. "If you don't leave, I'll get the police in here!"

More scuffling ensued. The booth's canvas shuddered and seemed ready to collapse.

Shannon rounded the corner and saw a slender man standing alone, gulping in deep breaths. She caught a flash of a woman who resembled Cassandra Presley slipping away between the booths, but Shannon hadn't seen her well enough to be sure of her identity.

"Can I help you?" the man asked.

Shannon nodded and read his name tag. "Do you work for Doggie Delights, Mr. Foote?"

"Yes," he answered, trying to control his rapid breathing. "Call me Lincoln, please."

"Very well, Lincoln. I'm Shannon. I wondered if you could tell me the name of the woman you were just arguing with."

He blinked at her. "And who are you exactly?"

Shannon explained that she was trying to solve Millicent's murder. "I heard the woman say something about a commercial and thought it might be the same commercial Scarlet had contracted."

He tipped his head to the side for a moment and ran his

eyes over Shannon. "I'm afraid this is none of your business. If you'll excuse me, I need to get back to work."

Shannon watched him turn away, then she faced Coleen. "I think he's genuinely afraid of that woman—and he has every reason to be if my suspicions about her are correct."

"Then you need to be careful." Coleen drew her mouth into a straight line and glanced at her watch. "I offered to help Joyce at the booth now, but I don't want you traipsing about the park, asking inflammatory questions all by yourself. Maybe you should ask Chief Grayson for help this morning."

Shannon shook her head. "Given my recent conversation with him, I don't think he'll listen to my theory. I don't have anything concrete to tell him. Not yet anyway."

Coleen settled her hands on her hips. "I don't like the look in your eye. What are you planning?"

Shannon held up the list she still clutched in one hand. "While it's still fresh in my mind, I'm going to find the two women on this list to see if their appearance or voice matches the woman who just ran off."

Coleen gripped Shannon's arm. "That could be dangerous."

Shannon patted her friend's hand. "I'll be fine. If I don't ask them any questions about Millicent, they won't know what I'm up to."

"Um, they might if one of them is the one who left that scary note on your windshield. Have you forgotten about that?"

"Hardly. Relax; I'm just going to make polite conversation. Nothing to it."

"Why do I fear it won't be that simple?" Coleen said, her voice drifting off as Shannon walked away.

— 19 —

Shannon had been so certain one of the women on her list of treat ball buyers would turn out to be the woman who'd verbally assaulted Mr. Foote about the Doggie Delights commercial, but she was wrong. It didn't take her long to learn that both of those women had departed the day before. So that left only Oliver Daniels and Cassandra as potential suspects in town to pursue.

With a sigh, Shannon lowered herself onto a bench outside the main tent and dug out the updated schedule. Cassandra's poodle, Fifi Maxim, had won her group and should have appeared in a showing thirty minutes earlier. If Shannon was lucky, the current round hadn't finished, and Cassandra would still be in the tent.

Gathering her resolve and mentally preparing herself for another chase, she rose and slipped inside the tent's front entrance. She stood on her toes and peered over the spectators at the middle ring. Three dogs, including Fifi, stood in the center. A gangly male judge studied them as their owners appeared to wait with bated breath.

"Congratulations to …" The judge paused for effect, and the captivated crowd waited in silence. "… the Pomeranian!"

The crowd erupted in applause, and disappointment claimed Cassandra's face for a moment before she flashed a taut smile. She tugged on Fifi's leash to bring her closer and then shook the winning owner's hand before making a beeline for the exit. Shannon darted outside and ran to the back exit, where she waited for Cassandra to emerge.

When Cassandra caught sight of Shannon, her eyes narrowed, and she quickly glanced around the tent as if looking for another means of escape.

"You can't avoid me forever," Shannon said.

Cassandra squared her shoulders, stepped forward and brushed Shannon out of the way. "Watch me."

Shannon caught up and stepped in Cassandra's path, again nodding toward Grayson, who hadn't left his earlier spot. "If you don't talk to me, I'm going to bring my friend Chief Grayson over here to talk to you instead, and he can be a real bear to deal with."

Thankfully, the bluff worked. Cassandra halted. "What do you want?"

Shannon pulled the woman and her dog out of the crowd. "You know I'm investigating Millicent's death. I simply want to rule you out as a suspect. If you're truly innocent in the matter, why do you keep running away from me?"

Cassandra pursed her lips.

"Fine. I'll get the chief." Shannon took a step.

"Wait." Cassandra stilled her with her hand. "I did something I'm not proud of, but I did *not* kill Millicent."

"What did you do?"

"Fifi didn't make the cut at the Doggie Delights show last month, but Scarlet did. Millicent desperately wanted to win, and she paid me to help her."

"Oh? What exactly did she pay you to do?"

"I spooked a dog as he entered the ring, so he wouldn't

show well," Cassandra said, nervously twisting Fifi's leash in her hand. "And he didn't. I cost him the competition."

Now we're getting somewhere. "Whose dog?"

"Linda Becker's Lab."

It wasn't a name Shannon recognized. "Is Linda here this weekend?"

"Yes," Cassandra said.

"Do you know where I can find her?"

Cassandra shook her head. "We're not exactly talking to each other anymore."

"She knows what you did?"

"Yes, and before you ask, I told her that Millicent paid me to do it."

"Is there anyone in the dog show world who wins honestly?" Shannon asked, completely disgusted by the dirty tricks employed by these owners.

Cassandra flinched. "I would never do anything like this if my husband hadn't lost his job. We were about to lose our home. Millicent paid me enough to make six months' worth of mortgage payments."

Shannon blinked. "That's a lot of money."

Fifi jumped up and pulled on her leash. Cassandra tugged back, and the dog lay down. "Millicent was convinced that if Scarlet won, she would get a commercial with Doggie Delights, and the money would have been well spent."

"I heard a woman talking to a man from Doggie Delights a few minutes ago," Shannon said, "and she mentioned something about losing out on the commercial."

"That was probably Linda. After Scarlet's contract for the commercial was announced, Linda told anyone who would listen that if her Lab had won, he'd have gotten that commercial instead of Scarlet." Cassandra's shoulders drooped. "I felt really bad about what I did, so I went to the Doggie Delights rep and asked him if that was why he chose Scarlet. He said that it wasn't the reason. He picked her because she was soft and cuddly, and their customers could relate to her."

"So even if Millicent hadn't played a trick so Scarlet could win, it wouldn't have made a difference in the commercial?"

"Exactly. But Linda didn't believe it, and she's hounded the Doggie Delights people at every show since then."

"Do you think it's likely that Linda killed Millicent?" Shannon asked.

Cassandra shook her head. "She showed her Lab in Portland Friday night and didn't get here until late Saturday morning." Fifi whined, and Cassandra patted her head. "If you'll excuse me, I need to feed Fifi."

"One more thing," Shannon said before Cassandra could take off. "Where were you between five and seven the night Millicent was killed?"

"Having dinner and drinks with Lilly Lansdown and Grace Givens."

"That's odd. When I talked with Lilly, she didn't mention that you were with them that night."

"I don't know why not. But check with both of them. They'll vouch for me." Cassandra jerked her dog's leash. "C'mon Fifi. Let's get something to eat and hit the road."

As they walked away, Shannon pondered her next move. *Next move—hah! My only move!*

She tugged her bag from her shoulder and pulled out

the schedule. Oliver Daniels's dog had been in the same round of competition with Fifi. Shannon hadn't noticed him in the tent, but she'd been preoccupied with Cassandra. He obviously hadn't made it to the top three, or he would've been standing center ring with Cassandra and Fifi.

Shannon headed back toward the tent. As she walked, her skin crawled with the feeling that someone was watching her again. She glanced behind her and met Grayson's stare.

"You're barking up the wrong tree with Cassandra," he called out.

Wondering why he was still leaning against the same tree since his talk with Kate, Shannon approached him. "No pun intended?"

"What?"

"*Barking* up the wrong tree. The dog show ..."

"Ah, didn't even realize what I said." He waved his hand absently. "I meant she couldn't have killed Millicent. Her alibi checks out."

"Have you—"

"Shannon!" Kate's excited voice rang out from behind. She ran up to Shannon and grabbed her arm. "C'mon. We have to go. Bye, Grayson."

"Where are we going?" Shannon asked as Kate pulled her down the sidewalk.

"That guy, Oliver Daniels, the one on your list—he's arguing with the Doggie Delights man right now."

"I guess everyone wanted that contract."

Shannon let Kate lead her down the walk to the Doggie Delights booth. Oliver stood red-faced in front of Lincoln Foote, who dramatically rolled his eyes.

"Don't roll your eyes at me!" Oliver shouted. "Millicent didn't deserve the commercial. She was nothing but a hypocrite. She ratted out a competitor for drugging a dog, and then she turned around and drugged *my* dog—like somehow she's above the rules! I would have won that competition if she hadn't."

Lincoln brushed him off. "And I've told you that the competition means nothing to us. Your bulldog would never be selected for our commercials. Cute, cuddly pets make people buy, not drooling, snout-faced bulldogs." Lincoln moved closer and glared at Oliver, which Shannon found foolhardy, as Oliver was powerfully built and Lincoln resembled a string bean.

"But now that Scarlet is missing, you must need a replacement." Oliver sounded desperate.

"If she doesn't turn up soon, we'll find another dog."

"My Spike is the perfect candidate, if you'd come take another look at him."

Lincoln wrapped his arms around his middle. "You and all the other owners are giving me an ulcer. I'm tired of you begging for Scarlet's spot. Your bulldog won't be selected, no matter what you do. Now, if you'll excuse me, I have a booth to run."

Oliver made a fist and swung at the sales rep, but Lincoln stepped aside before Oliver's fist made contact with his face. Irate, Oliver stood panting, his arm half-raised as if he might strike again. His sleeve slid back, revealing an angry bite on his forearm.

"Och! Look at his arm," Shannon whispered.

"A bite mark," Kate said, excitement in her voice.

"He's right-handed and tall enough to fit the medical examiner's criteria for the killer too."

"And he bought a treat ball! Plus, he's clearly got a nasty temper. Oh my gosh, do you know what this means?" Kate exclaimed in a loud whisper. "He could very well be our guy!"

"This isn't over," Oliver warned, letting his arm fall. He spit at the ground near Lincoln's shoe and then stormed off.

"We have to follow him," Shannon said, taking off before Kate could respond.

Kate caught up to her. "Maybe we should go get some help first."

"We don't have enough proof to get Grayson to act. Besides, we're in a crowd of people. Oliver won't hurt us." Shannon hurried to catch up with him. "Mr. Daniels!"

"What are you doing?" Kate hissed.

"Trying to slow him down."

He didn't turn but kept marching toward the back of the park. Slowed by the crowd, Shannon lost sight of him.

Dismayed, Shannon came to a stop. She shaded her eyes from the sun and scanned the area. "Where is he?"

"There." Kate pointed to the far side of the parking lot. "He's climbing into a motor home."

Shannon caught a glimpse of Oliver as he disappeared into an older-model, gray-and-white motor home with bright red stripes circling the body.

"Come on." Shannon said. "Let's go see what he's up to."

"The parking lot is deserted. It's not safe."

"He doesn't know we're onto him. For all he knows, we're out for a stroll."

"I don't know." Kate drew back.

Shannon patted her tote bag. "I have my phone right here. If we have any problems, we can call Grayson."

"I thought you said he wouldn't listen to you."

"He'll have to if a man is attempting to hurt us." Shannon linked her arm with Kate's and urged her forward before she could argue.

As they neared the lot, the door to the living quarters on the motor home burst open, and Oliver emerged. Shannon dragged Kate behind a stand of trees to watch. Oliver slammed and locked the door. He cast furtive glances around the area, and then he quickly raced across the grass.

"Perfect," Shannon said after he'd slipped past them. "Once he's out of sight, we can look in his windows."

Kate stared ahead. "They're covered with curtains."

"Maybe the ones in the back or other side aren't."

As soon as Oliver disappeared from sight, Shannon emerged from the trees and ran to the motor home. Up close, she noticed the dings and scrapes on the older vehicle. *Maybe Oliver needs money.* She peered inside through the passenger window, but couldn't see the back as he'd drawn a curtain across the living area.

"Let's check the other side." Shannon ran around the front, and Kate followed. She found two more windows, but both were covered. "Drat. Maybe we can see in the back."

"I'll look," Kate said, hurrying to the back. "No luck. The only window we can reach is cracked open, but the curtains are pulled."

Shannon joined her and chewed on her fingernail as she looked at the window. They needed to see inside, but breaking and entering wasn't a crime she was prepared to commit without any real evidence of Oliver's wrongdoing. She spied a dog sticker on the bumper giving her an idea.

"If Scarlet is inside and you call out to her, won't she respond to your voice?"

"Maybe."

"Try it."

Kate approached the window. "Scarlet," she called in a high voice. "Scarlet."

Other than the rustle of the wind through the trees, silence filled the air.

"Again," Shannon urged.

Kate stepped closer. "Scarlet. It's Kate. Are you in there, girl?"

Shannon held her breath. After a few moments, a soft whimper broke the quiet.

"Scarlet, is that you?" Encouraged, Kate called again, "Scarlet!"

The dog responded with a more excited whimper.

"She's here!" Shannon said.

"We can't be sure," Kate warned, but her excited expression declared the opposite. "Another dog could simply be responding."

"Do you think it's another dog?"

She hesitated, then shook her head. "No. I'm pretty sure it's Scarlet."

"Good." Shannon fought the urge to jump up and down and whoop with joy over finding the dog. "Now all we need to do is prove it."

"If we tell Grayson, he can get a warrant to search the motor home," Kate suggested.

"It's our best option." Shannon slapped a high five with Kate. "We could call him, but this isn't a life-or-death matter, and he can easily brush us off on the phone. After what happened at Rex's house, it's going to take a face-to-face plea to get him to come here—preferably by someone other than me. Can you go talk to him, and I'll keep an eye on the motor home in case Oliver comes back and tries to flee with Scarlet?"

"I can't leave you here alone," Kate replied.

"I'll be fine."

Kate stood, her eyes uncertain.

"Go!" Shannon said firmly. "Hurry, before Oliver comes back."

"Be careful." Kate hugged Shannon, then she bolted across the grass.

Excitement over their discovery sent adrenaline flooding through Shannon's veins. It was all she could do to stand still until the chief arrived. She remained behind the motor home, speaking reassuringly to Scarlet, telling her they were trying to rescue her. But as time ticked by, she began to worry that Kate hadn't been able to convince Chief Grayson to help them. After the fiasco at Rex Carrolton's house, he'd likely demanded proof that Oliver had Scarlet—not that Shannon could blame him.

But if that was true, then she needed to get the proof he required. She studied the motor home carefully. Oliver had left a set of curtains cracked open in the middle on a high window. A ladder ran from the bumper to the roof. If she climbed up, maybe she could lean to the side and snap a picture of Scarlet.

Shouldering her bag, she stepped up the rungs and hung precariously out from the ladder. She could see into a small bedroom area. Two dog crates sat next to each other at the foot of the bed. One held a brown dog, the other a white one. They'd curled into tight little balls, so even after seeing the flyers with Scarlet's picture on them, she couldn't positively identify the white one as Scarlet.

With any luck, an enlarged picture would allow Kate to make a positive ID. Shannon reached into her tote bag to retrieve her camera. Suddenly, the strap was jerked from her shoulder, pulling the bag and her body to the ground. She landed on her stomach, knocking the air out of her lungs.

"I warned you to leave this alone," a deep male voice said. "My note was perfectly clear."

— 20 —

Shannon rolled to her back and pushed up on her elbows. Oliver Daniels loomed over her, his angry eyes burning into her. She dug her feet into the grass and tried to slide back.

"If you'd only minded your own business," he said.

"I couldn't let you hurt Scarlet," Shannon blurted out, trying to catch her breath and buy time.

"Hurt her? Are you daft, woman? I'd never hurt a dog."

Shannon coughed. "But you'd kill a woman?"

She heard footsteps on the sidewalk along with people engaged in conversation. The footsteps drew closer. One heavy set thumped hard on the concrete. Another smaller, lighter set sounded like skipping. *A child?*

She opened her mouth to call out.

Oliver dropped to the ground and clamped his hand over her mouth. She struggled to free herself. He put a knee on her stomach, pinning her to the ground and then bent low. His sour breath fanned over her face. "If you try to get their attention, I'll hurt them too. I killed Millicent. What's a few more deaths on my hands?"

"Can we really get a puppy, Daddy?" a child's voice pleaded.

"We'll see," a man answered.

Shannon couldn't be responsible for someone else getting hurt. Especially not a child. She quit struggling and stared ahead. The footsteps continued down the sidewalk and gradually receded.

"Now what am I going to do with you?" Oliver asked. "You know about Millicent, so I can't let you go."

With his clammy hand still pressed over her mouth, Shannon knew he wasn't open to her suggestions. His gaze darted back and forth, and suddenly his eyes lit with excitement. He let go of her mouth and grabbed a leash hanging from the bumper of his motor home.

"Let's take a little ride, shall we?" He flipped her over and wrapped the braided nylon around her wrists, jerking it tight.

Pain radiated up her arm, and she winced.

"Bet you wish you'd taken my warning seriously now, eh?" He jerked her to her feet and dragged her to the motor home's side door.

"Help! Somebody!" Shannon screamed as loud as she could, searching the area for Kate, but she didn't see her or Grayson.

Where are you, Kate?

"Get in there!" Oliver gave her a savage shove up the steps and through the doorway. Her foot caught on a throw rug by the door, and she stumbled the rest of the way in.

Jostled by the commotion, the dogs stood up in their crates. She hoped they'd break into a barking frenzy and help to alert anyone in the area of her situation. Instead, they quizzically tilted their heads sideways and watched. From everything Kate had told Shannon about well-trained dogs, their submissive behavior shouldn't have surprised her.

Oliver quickly drew the door closed behind them. "If you dare scream one more time, I will kill you where you stand."

Shannon looked into his eyes, and her scream died in her throat. He wasn't bluffing.

"Good girl." Oliver pressed the lock into place with a resounding click and then pointed at a captain's chair behind the front seats. "Now sit." He said it as if Shannon was some kind of show dog.

With her legs still trembling from the adrenaline rush, she obeyed, her mind racing. Out of the corner of her eye, she noticed the dogs do the same, and she fought the crazy urge to laugh at the absurdity of the situation. The well-worn motor home smelled musty and pungent—like wet dogs. Shannon's eyes searched for a way to escape. The quarters were tight. If she made a move, he'd be on her in a second.

Oliver pulled a long leash out of a cabinet. He tied it around her and the seat. "This ought to hold you."

Her heart filled with dread. "What are you going to do to me?"

"Well, sweet cakes, it seems to me there's only one way to keep you from telling anyone about me." He knotted the leash around her chest and jerked it tight. "You have to die. Like Millicent."

"You won't get away with this." Panic sent the words flying from her mouth. "My friend was here, and she knows you have Scarlet. She's gone to get the police."

"We'll be long gone before she gets back here."

"She'll describe your motor home. With a vehicle of this size, there's no way you can hide."

"Hmm, good point. We'll lay low until dark. And I know of the perfect spot—it even has a great ocean view." He turned back to the cupboard and pulled out a bright blue bandana. "I can't have you crying out for help."

Shannon eyed the dirty bandana. "There's no need for that. I promise I won't scream."

"Sure you won't." He twirled the fabric into a narrow strip.

She bit down on her lips, but he scissored the fabric between them and knotted the bandanna in the back.

He jumped into the driver's seat and dug a worn map out of the console. "A quick look at the map to find the day use park and we'll be off."

He mumbled the directions, and Shannon realized she was familiar with the park where he was taking her. It was usually deserted, as people rarely used it—but at least it was still in the Apple Grove area. More chance of Grayson finding them before it was too late.

He stowed the map and then fired up the powerful engine.

Shannon rubbed her cheek against her shoulder to try to loosen the bandana, but the foul-tasting cloth wouldn't budge. The depressing thought occurred to her that she might survive Oliver only to die of some lethal brain-eating virus living in the material.

"Let's get out of here." Oliver shifted into gear and pressed the gas pedal.

The motor home bounced out of the parking lot and onto Main Street. People filled the sidewalks, and Shannon saw Coleen walking with Melanie. She tried to yell, but the gag muffled the sound. *I have to get free!* She frantically fought against her restraints. The cords bit into her arms but didn't give an inch.

"They can't see or hear you, you know," Oliver said,

satisfaction in his tone. "You might as well relax and enjoy the ride."

He stopped at a four-way intersection, and she continued to try to loosen the bandana with her shoulder. She felt it inch upward, but the dry cotton still clung to her mouth. When the traffic eased, their vehicle cleared the intersection and rumbled down the street. On the outskirts of town, Oliver took a left on Old Beach Trail. They bumped over potholes, sending items in the cupboards banging loudly.

Shannon prayed for someone to be in the park, but as she'd predicted, the small space surrounded by tall dunes and grasses was completely deserted. Oliver maneuvered the vehicle backward into the small parking area, well hidden from the road. Then he shifted into park and killed the engine.

"Now we kick back and wait for the sun to go down." Glancing at his watch, he swiveled his chair to face her. "We have a few hours yet."

Shannon couldn't stand to have the gag in her mouth for another minute. She furrowed her brows and grunted at him.

He sighed. "I suppose it wouldn't hurt to take that out while no one's around." He scooted over to her and untied the fabric.

"Yuck," she croaked out between dry lips, trying to get the taste out of her mouth.

"It's getting hot in here." He pushed up his shirt-sleeves and reached up to crank open a skylight. Then he propped open the main door. Sunlight brightened the dismal space, and the stale air began to flow away with the briny winds. "Try any funny stuff and the gag goes back in—tighter this time."

Shannon nodded, spitting out fuzzies. Or possibly dog hair.

"You must be thirsty." He grabbed a bottle of water from the refrigerator. "Just because I'm going to kill you doesn't mean I'm uncivilized." He poured water into a cup with a straw and held it up for her to drink.

She wanted to refuse on principle, but that would be foolish. The water cooled her parched throat. "Since this is to be my last meal, might I also have something to eat?" she asked. "Perhaps something from a drive-through?"

"Nice try." He moved to the small table and sipped his water. "So how did you figure out I had Scarlet anyway?"

"Millicent never let Scarlet have a treat ball, and you left one by her crate."

He swung his legs like he didn't have a care in the world. "That doesn't tie her to me."

"We figured whoever took her would buy a new treat ball to keep Scarlet occupied. You were one of three owners who purchased one from my friend Kate. After hearing your argument with the man from Doggie Delights and seeing the bite mark on your arm, we figured you were the person who murdered Millicent. When we found your motor home, Kate called through the open window for Scarlet. She whimpered, and we knew we were right."

He tossed his empty water bottle in the sink. "Could have been any dog whimpering."

"Kate knows Scarlet well, so she recognized Scarlet's whimper. I'm sure once we involve the police, they'll be able to prove the blood found by the crate came from the bite on your arm. They'll also find your prints on the treat ball."

"Hmm, it's too bad you're not there to tell them all of this. Instead, here we are. You all tied up, and me in the driver's seat—literally." He laughed wickedly at his bad joke.

"Kate will tell them. She knows everything too."

"I'll deal with that if it really happens." He studied her. "I suspect you're bluffing about your 'friend' who knows so much."

Shannon decided to take another approach. "It's strange; you didn't strike me as the type to murder someone when I first met you."

He shrugged. "Killing Millicent changed me—made me feel freer. More alive, ironically."

"I don't understand."

"I didn't mean to kill her," he said offhandedly. "But once I did, I realized *I* had the power to stop people from taking control of my life. I felt more powerful. More in charge of my destiny. Like nothing can ever best me again."

"Really? What about the man from Doggie Delights? It didn't sound like you were in charge of that conversation."

His eyes narrowed into snakelike slits. "He'll pay for that."

"You're going to kill him too?"

"Won't be necessary. I've learned he has a gambling problem, and I intend to blackmail him into giving Spike the commercial."

"Ah. That sounds good in theory, but the fact is, you aren't very good at this kidnapping-and-murder thing." Shannon shrugged. "You'll be in jail long before you get the chance to do that."

Oliver shot to his feet, nearly hitting his head on the roof. "You can't talk to me like that! No one talks to me like that anymore!" He leaned over her, his expression fierce, and his fingers coiled around her neck.

"Och!" She tried to back away, but his fingers tightened. His eyes glazed over, and his fingers clamped down like a vise.

— 21 —

Darkness swam before Shannon's eyes. She felt the strange desire to give in and float away, to end the impossible struggle for air, but she refused to succumb to it.

"No," she croaked out with a strangled breath. "Wait."

"Give me a good reason to stop." His fingers slackened, but he didn't back away.

She drew in as much air as she could, her chest rising and falling from the exertion as she searched for a reason why he should let her live. Why would he need her? An idea floated into her oxygen-deprived brain.

"If the police find you here," she said, her voice scratchy. She cleared her throat. "You may need a hostage."

He thought it over and then fully retracted his fingers. "Don't talk to me like that again, or I won't stop next time. Understand?"

She nodded and gulped in air. Small-town life in America was not turning out to be the peaceful experience she'd expected.

Oliver took a step back and ran a shaky hand through his hair. Although he professed to be a merciless killer, judging by the way his hand shook, Shannon thought he might still have a shred of humanity left.

Which meant there was still hope.

He dropped into the driver's seat and leaned it back.

Propping his hands behind his head, he silently stared at the roof.

Shannon quietly scooted away from the back of the chair as far as her restraints allowed and worked her hands back and forth, finally loosening the leash enough to dig her fingers into the knot. Her spirits soared at the small gain, and she started working at the knot with her fingernails. When she heard soft snoring coming from Oliver, she was so relieved that she nearly burst out in giddy laughter. She wisely stifled it and continued to claw at the leash. As the sun dropped below the horizon, her fingers felt like they could fall off at any moment, but she still kept at it. A few more minutes, and she'd be free.

The bulldog started barking, and Oliver shifted in his seat. He blinked rapidly for a moment before quickly standing. "What's the matter, boy? You need to go out?"

The dog barked harder, and his feet clicked against the base of his crate as if he were dancing.

On his way to the crate, Oliver stopped next to Shannon and patted her on the head as if she were a puppy. "It's getting dark. A quick trip outside for the doggies, and we'll be on our way."

He strolled to the back of the motor home, and she focused every bit of her energy on working the knots. She heard the crate doors open and excited little feet skipping across the linoleum floor. Soon they all disappeared outside, giving her the perfect chance to escape.

Her fingers clawed frantically at the leash. The knot had moved a fraction of an inch. She wiggled it harder and was certain she was mere moments from freeing herself.

The door jerked open, and she let out a muffled cry of dismay.

No! He can't be back so soon.

"Honey, I'm home," Oliver called out, chuckling to himself.

She felt the vehicle move as he stepped inside and closed the door. He took his time settling the dogs in their crates and giving them water. She worked her finger harder. *So close.*

Oliver stopped in the kitchen, stowed items in cabinets, and then locked drawers and doors. After latching the refrigerator, he strutted to the driver's seat.

I have to stall him.

"Oliver, you claim that you didn't mean to kill Millicent," Shannon said, continuing to work the leash behind her back. "So why did you?"

"Initially, my plan was only to steal Scarlet. That way she wouldn't be able to fulfill the contract for the commercial, and Doggie Delights would sign Spike instead. It was a cut-and-dried plan of revenge to get back at Millicent for drugging my dog and stealing our trophy. When I got to town, I staked out Millicent's house and waited for her to leave so I could snatch Scarlet." He shook his head. "But Millicent forgot something and came back. She caught me in the act and threatened to have me arrested."

"Wouldn't it have been better to be charged with dog-napping than murder?"

"I'm an attorney. If I'm convicted of any crime, I could be disbarred." He turned the keys in the ignition, and the engine roared to life.

No. I need more time.

"I tried to talk her out of it," he continued as he shifted into gear. "But as usual, she wouldn't listen. I couldn't let her ruin my life when she was the one who'd caused me to lose the competition in the first place. As she left the room to call the police, I grabbed the closest thing and hit her over the head." He glanced back at Shannon, a snide grin on his face. "It was just icing on the cake that it happened to be the Doggie Delights trophy. It was kind of like she killed herself, if you know what I mean."

Right …

"I also stole one of her precious little figurines," he said. "I figure I can get a pretty good price for it online."

He pressed the gas pedal, and the motor home lurched forward. Shannon dug harder with her index finger. It finally slid through the knot. She curled it toward her palm, and the knot gave way. She quickly worked down the loops until her hands were blessedly free. Slowly, she brought them down to her sides. Her shoulder muscles rebelled, clamping into tight knots, but she bit her lip to wait out the cramp.

What now? I can't fling myself out the door at sixty miles per hour.

She peered out the window. The road curved about a mile ahead, and he'd have to slow to make the curve. The speed would still be too fast for her to bail, but she had to do something before they reached the main road leading into the mountains. Her only hope of stopping him now was to try to turn off the key and hope the vehicle would slow enough for her to escape.

She returned her focus to Oliver, who was busy humming a

creepy version of a nursery rhyme. Four simple steps and she'd be on him. With no time to waste, she loosened the leash that held her to the chair and lunged forward, thrusting her hand toward the key.

"What the—" He looked up and karate-chopped her hand.

She held firm and twisted the key. The engine stilled, and she jerked the key out so he couldn't restart the vehicle.

He took one hand from the wheel and grabbed her wrist. The motor home hit a bump, and she flew toward the passenger door. The vehicle slid onto the shoulder, the tires spitting gravel that pinged on the underbelly.

Yelling, he released his grip on her and grabbed the wheel. Overcorrecting, he caused the vehicle to careen across the road and then back the other way.

"Gah!" Shannon tumbled into the aisle, hitting her head on a console box.

The vehicle swerved back and forth in growing arcs until it hit the shoulder hard. Gravel took the tires and pulled them toward the ditch. Shannon wrapped her arms around the dining table's metal base and prepared for impact.

One side of the vehicle hit a tree. Metal crumpled and groaned. The motor home teetered, and with a loud grinding of metal, it fell onto the driver's side like an aluminum can thrown into a recycle bin. Shannon's back slammed into the wall. The dogs yelped. She prayed and held on with all her strength until the big tin can slid to a stop.

Dazed, she waited for everything in the motor home to quit shaking before she crawled away from the table. She saw Oliver still belted in his seat, but he wasn't moving. The crates had settled at the back of the vehicle. The bewildered dogs had already stood up on what was usually the side of their crates and were watching her with keen eyes. Neither of them looked hurt, but they seemed to be as dazed as she was.

She shook her head to clear it and made her way into the aisle. The exit door was now positioned on the ceiling. Hopefully, she would be able to stand on the table and hoist herself out. But first, she needed to know if there was any chance Oliver would be coming after her. She pulled herself atop the refrigerator, which was now on the floor, and looked down on him. He wasn't moving, and a heavy coating of blood covered his head. Leaning closer, she could see his leg was pinned by the steering column. She also spotted smoke coming from the engine.

Fire?

She had to get out. But she couldn't leave the dogs to die in a fire—or Oliver, no matter how tempting.

With fear inching up her spine, Shannon reached up for the door and shoved hard. It flew open but came crashing right back down. She tried again. Same problem. She wasn't strong enough to throw it all the way open. As the smell of smoke snaked into the vehicle, panic crept into her heart.

A window. She had to try a window. And quickly.

Crawling to the back of the vehicle, she climbed over the dog crates and shoved the mattress out of the way. The caustic odor of gasoline rose up to meet her. Had they ruptured the gas tank? If so, the engine fire could catch and quickly consume the whole vehicle.

I have to hurry!

She quickly pried open the window and punched out the

screen. Then she crawled back to get Scarlet. She got the crate open and pulled the terrified dog out by her harness.

"Come on. That's a good girl," Shannon cooed as she made her way back to the window. She leaned out as far as she could and lowered Scarlet to the ground. Shannon did the same thing for Spike. Once out of the motor home, both dogs stood with heads cocked to the side and looked up at her expectantly.

"Sorry, you two. I have one more rescue before I can join you." She heard a whoosh outside and saw the grass catch fire.

Terrified, she scrambled back inside. Smoke seeped into the space through crevices. She had one chance to save Oliver before it was too late. She crawled toward him, found the filthy bandana, and tied it over her nose and mouth.

"I need you to wake up, Oliver," she said loudly as she approached. He didn't stir. She braced her legs between the seats and tried to move the steering column. It wouldn't budge. She reached over Oliver and grabbed the lever to move his seat back. It slid a few inches, and he groaned in pain.

She heard a hiss of air behind her and saw the curtains catch fire. Smoke quickly filled the small space. Her eyes watered from the caustic fumes, and she struggled for air. There was no time to help Oliver.

Coughing, she looked around for the quickest means of escape.

Due to the flames, the rear window exit was no longer an option. She'd have to go out the front. She cranked the passenger window down, each turn of the crank straining her oxygen supply. Her body getting weak, she reached for the open window and pulled herself up. Her arms gave way, and she collapsed on the exterior of the vehicle with only her head and chest outside.

C'mon, Shannon. You can do this. Only a few more feet to go.

She reached out for anything to latch onto, but her hands came up empty. Smoke billowed up to meet her. She tried not to panic, but she couldn't breathe. The world started spinning, and her vision blurred before everything faded to black.

— 22 —

Large hands tugged Shannon's body over hot metal as a deep male voice tried to pierce her thoughts. She heard only gibberish, and the feeling of floating filled her senses. She was at the end of a deep tunnel with miles to travel before she'd be able to make out the words. Hands lifted and strong arms secured her body. The man moved quickly, jostling her as he ran. His voice grew more insistent, and she finally gave in, drifting toward the sound.

"Open your eyes, Shannon," the man demanded as he settled her on soft grass.

She blinked. "Michael?"

He sighed out a breath of relief. "You were trapped in the motor home. I have to leave you to get the other person out, but an ambulance is on the way."

Oliver ... the dogs ... the fire.

"Go," she tried to give the word urgency, but it whispered out in a coughing fit.

Michael jumped up and disappeared from her view. She let her lids fall and felt the tunnel pull her back. *No!* She wouldn't go back there. Forcing her eyes open, she tried to lift her head to locate Michael, but she didn't have enough strength to keep it raised. With her last remaining strength, she pulled her body back and upward until she rested against the rough bark of a tree.

She saw Michael disappear into the motor home through the same window she'd used for escape. The back half of the vehicle burned in bright flames, their tips reaching up to the lowest branches of the trees. The leaves crackled as they caught fire, and the sky lit up with vivid reds and oranges.

Oh, please keep Michael safe, she prayed.

A siren wailed in the distance. Soon an emergency vehicle rounded the corner, the glow of its lights twirling and mixing with that of the blaze. The ambulance screeched to a halt, and two medics leapt out, heading straight for Shannon.

"No," she shouted, her voice hoarse. "Two men. In the motor home. Help them."

The medics reversed course. As they pounded across the grass, the upper half of Oliver's body was pushed through the motor home's passenger window, and he lay facedown in the exact spot where Shannon had collapsed not long ago.

The EMTs pulled him out, and they rushed him away from the blaze. Michael's strong hands shot up and grabbed the door handle, hauling his body up and over the frame. He ran from the fire, stopping near the EMTs to lean over and plant his hands on his knees. Shannon saw him strain for deep breaths and heard him coughing as fresh air settled into his lungs.

"You need oxygen," an EMT said from where he knelt over Oliver.

"Treat this guy and Shannon first. I'm fine." He stood and drew in more air, his gaze landing on her. He walked toward her, residual coughing making him stop a few times to catch his breath. In the distance, another siren spiraled closer.

"You should let the paramedics look at you," she said when he reached her.

"It's only a little smoke." He squatted next to her. "You're looking like you have more color."

"Thanks to you."

"Can you tell me what happened?"

She tried to tell him about Oliver and the motor home, but the adrenaline that had fueled her up until that moment ebbed away now that she knew Michael was safe. She suddenly felt too weary to keep her eyes open.

"Later," she whispered. And she let the darkness claim her again.

*   *   *

An insistent beeping pulled Shannon from a deep sleep. She reached for her nightstand to turn off the alarm. Her fingers brushed an empty table. Where was that incessant alarm? She opened one eye, but a bright light burned into her retina, and she closed it again. She ignored the beep and focused on her scratchy throat. Something covered her mouth. She reached up and found a plastic mask.

What in the world ...?

"She's awake!" Coleen's excited voice sounded from somewhere nearby.

Shannon pulled off the mask. "Coleen? What are you doing in my room?"

"You're in the hospital, honey."

Shannon forced her eyes open, squinting to keep the bright light at bay. Coleen and Kate stood at one side of her bed; Betty, Joyce, and Melanie at the other side. All wore identical concerned expressions. Shannon tried to remember what had brought her here, but her mind was filled with fog.

"Why am I here?" she asked.

Kate took her hand. "Oliver Daniels kidnapped you. I tried to get help, but he took off with you before I could get back. I'm so sorry."

Memories flooded Shannon's mind. The motor home. The fire. Dogs yipping. Oliver pinned behind the wheel. Michael rescuing them both.

"Is Michael here too? Is he OK?" She tried to sit up. The room spun.

"Easy." Betty placed a warm hand on Shannon's shoulder and gently eased her back against the pillow.

Coleen squeezed her hand. "Michael's fine. He's been treated and released."

"And Oliver?"

"The doctors say Oliver will recover fully," Coleen said gruffly.

"And he'll spend the rest of his life behind bars, thanks to you," Kate said, her voice filled with gratitude. "I don't know how I can ever thank you for what you did."

"There's no need. That's what friends are for," Shannon said. "I'm glad Oliver survived—despite everything he put me through."

"Speaking of that deranged lunatic, are you up to telling us what happened with Oliver?" Coleen asked.

"Can I have some water first?"

"Of course you can." Coleen poured water into a plastic cup while Joyce helped Shannon sit up. Kate fluffed the pillows, and Shannon smiled over her friends' fussing. She took a long sip of the water, and her throat felt a bit better.

She handed the glass to Coleen and launched into her story, telling her friends all about the kidnapping, Oliver's admission to killing Millicent, and how she switched off the motor home's ignition key. "Then I got the dogs out and tried to free Oliver, but the smoke got too thick. The next thing I remember was Michael carrying me to the grass."

"He was so worried about you," Coleen said. "He refused treatment for himself and rode in the ambulance with you."

"He's been worried sick about you since I first told him you were missing," Kate added.

"How did he find me, anyway?" Shannon asked.

Kate's eyes clouded over. "I went to tell Grayson about finding Scarlet. He and I were on our way to meet you when we ran into Michael. By the time we made it back to the parking lot, the motor home was gone and so were you." Kate shook her head. "I was so worried for you. Especially when we found your phone and your bag."

"You should've seen Michael. He was like your knight in shining armor." Coleen's expression turned dreamy. "He got Chief Grayson to issue an alert on the motor home. Then he rounded up all the people who were still at the show and organized a search party."

"He did?" Shannon asked.

"M-hm. Most everyone figured Oliver had gotten you out of town. But not Michael. When others gave up, he staked out the road that led out of town in case Oliver tried to leave. Luckily, Scarlet came running down the road, and Michael knew you were close by."

"So you found Scarlet. How about Spike?" Shannon tried to take a deep breath, bringing on a coughing fit.

"You should put the oxygen back on." Betty settled the mask over Shannon's mouth.

"Both dogs are fine," Kate said. "They're at my house."

Shannon smiled, though no one could see behind the mask. A phone vibrated on the table.

"That's your phone," Kate said picking it up. "We brought it with us. Do you want to talk to anyone?"

Hoping Michael was calling, Shannon took the phone from Kate. She saw her mother's name on the screen and lifted up her mask to answer. "Hi, Beth."

"Shannon, thank goodness! Are you all right?"

"I'm fine," Shannon said, wondering how her mother had already heard she was in the hospital.

"I'd like to come by for a few minutes, if you're up to having visitors. I could bring the twins with me too."

"I'd love that," Shannon said.

"We'll see you all in an hour or so." Beth said goodbye and disconnected.

Coleen took the phone and placed it on the table. "Now it's time for us to get out of here so you can get some rest."

Shannon nodded, and her eyes drifted closed before her friends had left the room.

Much later, she woke with a start, feeling as if someone was watching her. She opened her eyes to find Michael standing over her bed, his face awash with remorse.

"Your mother and the twins were here," he told her. "They went to get some coffee and said they'd come back later."

Shannon lifted her oxygen mask. "I'm glad you stopped by. I wanted to thank you for being there when I needed you—again."

His jaw clenched. "You need to stop taking so many risks."

"Well, I don't go looking for danger, you know."

"But it sure finds you, doesn't it?" he said softly, looking down.

"It's hard for me to do nothing while watching the people I care about suffer," she said passionately, hoping he'd understand where she was coming from—that helping those she cared about meant the world to her.

"Your friends wouldn't want you to help if it meant you could lose your life. People who care deeply about you wouldn't knowingly put you in harm's way."

She studied him. "You're still upset about what happened in Portland last night."

"Of course I'm still upset," he said. "If I hadn't put you in that situation, you wouldn't have gotten hurt."

"What you did was invite me to accompany you to an otherwise lovely dinner. Being attacked by a crazed man wasn't on the agenda. It's not your fault that it happened." She smiled, trying to lighten his mood. "It was the luck of the draw."

"The reality is, I deal with some very unscrupulous people in my line of work." He clamped a hand on the back of his neck. "I should've realized something like this would happen. I know better."

She watched him carefully, weighing his comments until the sad truth dawned on her. "So your plan is to live the rest of your life in a self-imposed shell, as if someone is always waiting around the corner, plotting to harm you or the people you care about?"

He didn't respond. Shannon knew he was thinking of his late wife. He would forever blame himself for her death.

"That's not living, Michael." She waited for him to say something, but when he looked away, she got the message loud and clear. Michael was determined to keep her at arm's length. It was his way of protecting her. Surprisingly, the thought made her sadder than she imagined it would.

"Knock, knock," Coleen said from the open doorway. "I hope I'm not interrupting."

"Not at all." Michael stepped back from the bed. "I was just leaving."

"Thanks again for all that you did today," Shannon said. Their gazes locked for a moment before he nodded and walked away. Shannon knew from her own struggle over losing John that Michael still hadn't put his past behind him. Running away was the only thing he could do until he resolved his feelings of loss and guilt.

"Phew." Coleen ran her fingers across her forehead. "You could cut the tension in this room with a knife. What's going on?"

Tears pricked Shannon's eyes. She tipped her face to the ceiling.

"That's OK. Tell me when you're ready." Coleen settled on the bed and handed Shannon a tissue.

Shannon dabbed her tears. "He's not over losing his wife."

"Not over her? How can that be when it's obvious he's so interested in you?"

"Let me rephrase that. He's afraid of getting too close to someone for fear it might cause them to be hurt—or worse—due to his line of work."

A clear dawning broke in Coleen's eyes. "And here I was, practically throwing you at him." Coleen sat back. "I'm so sorry. If I'd known he felt this way, I wouldn't have been so pushy."

Shannon threw back her head and laughed until she coughed.

"What's so funny?" Coleen handed Shannon her water.

"You don't know yourself very well."

Coleen planted a hand on her hip. "What's that supposed to mean?"

"It means nothing is going to stop you from being pushy. That's who you are." Shannon smiled. "And I love you for it."

"Och, I'm so glad to have someone who will put up with me—beside my Ewan, that is." Coleen smiled fondly at the thought of her husband.

"Speaking of Ewan," Shannon said, "you haven't told me how long you're staying."

Coleen chuckled. "I figured you'd be ready to get rid of me in a week, so that's when my flight is booked."

"I'll never be ready to get rid of you." Tears threatened again. "But if you have to leave in a few days, you can at least tell me when I'll see you again."

"That's a good question. Ewan says he doesn't like it when I leave him alone for too long. But between you and me, I think he rather enjoys rambling around the house on his own now and again. Until he runs out of food, that is."

Shannon frowned.

"What's that look for?" Coleen asked.

"I miss being married."

Coleen's eyebrow shot up. "Does that mean you're officially in the market for a husband?"

"Officially, I would say ..." Shannon paused to draw out her answer. "I'm open to the possibility. But after last night's fiasco, I might not be dating again any time soon."

"I have a hunch Michael will come around."

"Perhaps."

"And if he doesn't, he isn't the only devilishly handsome fish in the sea." Coleen winked.

"I agree—and if another man ever asks me out, I might even go."

"Maybe I should stay a bit longer then." A broad grin spread across Coleen's face.

Shannon laughed. "It's not like there's anyone waiting in line to take me out."

Coleen's smile fell. "That's why you need me here." She pulled Shannon into a hug. "I miss you so much when we're apart."

"I miss you too." Shannon hugged back until she saw the nurse step into the room.

The nurse eyed Coleen. "It's time for Mrs. McClain to get some rest."

Coleen stood and sauntered toward the door. Over her shoulder, she said, "About my next visit—keep the tea handy. I suspect I'll be popping back in before you know it."

With a wink, she was gone.

Turn the page for an exclusive preview
of the next mystery in the
Creative Woman Mysteries series.

Patchwork of Lies

COMING SOON!

— 1 —

Shannon McClain awoke to the sound of a burglary in progress. After a long morning of helping her friend, Betty Russo, get ready for an onslaught of guests at The Apple Grove Inn, she had lain on the couch in the little room used to store furniture next to the inn's office. She'd only intended to rest her eyes. Instead, she'd fallen into a deep sleep. A full day of getting everything organized for the quilting workshops Betty planned to facilitate during the Apple Festival had left Shannon exhausted.

At first, Shannon couldn't comprehend what the odd scratching and thumping sounds in the room next to her meant. She opened her eyes, straining to hear through the wall. A drawer slid open and slammed shut. She sat up, wondering if Tom and Betty had returned home early from grocery shopping.

As she listened to someone banging around in the office, the hairs on the back of her neck prickled. Instinctively she knew it wasn't Tom or Betty.

Shannon rose from the sofa, treading lightly across the carpeted floor. She eased the door open. A narrow sliver of the office came into view as the noise, stomping and a rapid opening and closing of drawers, increased in intensity.

Her breath caught in her throat.

She saw broad shoulders and a dark hood drawn up over

the head—probably a man. With his back turned to her, the intruder rifled through file cabinet drawers.

Shannon pushed the door fully open and stood paralyzed as her heart thumped a mile a minute. *What can I do?* She'd left her cellphone in another room. The office phone rested only inches away from where the man frantically searched through drawers.

Steeling herself against her rising fear, she cleared her throat. In the strongest voice she could manage, she said, "What are you doing in here?"

The man turned, his head bent down. He bolted toward the door. On instinct, Shannon stepped forward to block his escape. He barreled into her, knocking her to the floor. Stunned from the impact, it took her a moment to recover. As she scrambled to her feet, she heard a back door open and slam shut. She raced after the intruder.

She struggled for a deep breath as she searched the trees behind the inn and surrounding property. No sign of the man. No one sitting on the patio chairs. The few guests who were already checked in were probably napping in their rooms or had gone into town. Shannon turned, pressing her hand against her back where it had impacted with the floor. It hurt every time she took a breath.

She hurried back to the office. Her hand shook as she picked up the phone to call Chief Grayson.

"Apple Grove police, Chief Grayson speaking."

She pressed the phone hard against her ear. "Grayson, it's Shannon McClain. I'm over at The Apple Grove Inn." She couldn't hide the tremble in her voice.

"Shannon, has something happened?"

The commanding strength of Grayson's voice calmed her nerves. "Someone broke into the Russos' office. I caught him in the act, but he got away."

"How long ago did this happen?"

"Not more than five minutes ago." Shannon paused for a breath, still winded from the pursuit.

"Which way did he run?" Grayson's voice remained steady.

Shannon turned in a semicircle and gazed at the door that led to the patio. "He ran out the back door, toward the grove of trees behind the inn."

"Tell me anything you can about what he looked like."

She closed her eyes. Her heart had slowed down to near normal, but her hands still vibrated. "Ummm ... I didn't get a look at his face. He wore a dark hoodie."

"I'll send an officer to search the area and the streets on the other side of those trees. And Shannon, you sit tight. I'll be right over." Compassion filled his voice.

"Thank you."

After placing the phone in its cradle, Shannon collapsed into the office chair. As she sat studying the open drawers and scattered papers, she noticed a foreign scent lingering in the air. She breathed more deeply, realizing that the distinct woodsy smell had been most intense when the intruder had knocked her over. *It must be the burglar's cologne.*

At the sound of the siren, she leaped to her feet and headed toward the front of the inn. Betty and Tom's sedan pulled into the driveway just ahead of the police SUV. Betty pushed the passenger side door open and stepped toward the house, holding a bag of groceries. The stiffness in her stride indicated that her arthritis might be acting up. She glanced at the police vehicle and then at Shannon, her eyes growing wide with unspoken questions.

Shannon swooped down the steps and put an arm around her friend. "I caught a man in your office. I tried to stop him." She managed to keep her voice calm.

Betty let out a sharp breath. She touched her palm to her chest.

Tom skirted the front of the car to stand beside his wife. "We were robbed?" He gripped the bag of groceries tighter.

"He opened a bunch of drawers. I'm not sure if he took anything." The look of shock on Tom and Betty's faces crushed Shannon. If only she had anticipated being knocked over, she might have been able to catch the guy. "I tried to stop him."

Chief Grayson opened his car door. His boots pounded the concrete as he lumbered toward them. "Why don't we go inside and talk?"

"I'll take care of the groceries, Bets." Tom took the bag from Betty and disappeared inside.

Shannon squeezed Betty's shoulder in a sideways hug and led her up the stairs. They stepped into the lobby with Chief Grayson taking up the rear.

Grayson shoved his hands into his pockets, glancing around the lobby and into the empty tearoom. "Quiet this time of day."

Betty responded after a moment, a dazed look in her eyes, "I wanted the place mostly empty today, so it would be easier to get it ready for the big crowd." She combed her fingers through her curly auburn hair. "With the Apple Festival starting tomorrow, we'll be full up by tonight. People made reservations months ago."

"The office is on the far side of the inn, away from the guest rooms," Shannon said as she treaded across the plush carpet.

"What were you doing here, Shannon?" Grayson paced the lobby, running his hand over the back of a Victorian-style couch done in a rich floral fabric. "With all the craft vendors in the park and everything else going on for the festival, I'd think you'd be plenty busy at the Paisley Craft Market."

Shannon stopped and turned to face Grayson. "We *are* very busy at my store." The whole town buzzed in anticipation of the festival. "But Betty needed to do a lot of extra preparation for the workshops, so I offered to help her out."

Though she'd only lived in Apple Grove a short time, Shannon felt a loyalty to Betty. Betty was the first person in Apple Grove to befriend her after she'd traveled all the way from Wainscott, Scotland, to claim her inheritance from her grandmother—a mansion with a summer house and the craft market. Despite the fact that they'd never met, Victoria Paisley had been generous to her granddaughter.

The chief turned toward Betty, now seated on a couch in the lobby. The worry lines on her forehead intensified. "Betty, I'm going to need your input too," he said. "Perhaps you can help us figure out what he took or what he meant to steal. Try not to disturb anything. We'll get a deputy over here to dust for prints."

Betty managed a nod, though the dazed expression of stunned disbelief remained. Once they entered the office,

Shannon talked the police chief through what had happened. She strode across the room, pointing out where she'd been standing when the intruder knocked her over.

"I wonder what he wanted in here." Grayson put his beefy hands on his police utility belt and turned to Shannon. "Did you notice if he held anything as he ran away?"

Shannon closed her eyes and pictured the thief barreling toward her. *Was anything in his hands?* It had all happened so fast. She shook her head. "I'm not sure."

Betty wandered around the room, growing paler by the minute. Her hand covered her mouth as her eyes glazed.

Shannon's heart broke over what her friend must be feeling. This couldn't be easy for her.

Betty gazed at the papers flung all over the floor, the open photo album on the desk, and the gaping drawers. "It doesn't look like anything is missing." She peered inside one of the drawers. "The petty cash box is still here."

An image flashed through Shannon's head of the thief shoving something in his pocket. Could she trust her memory? "He might have taken something small; I'm not sure what."

Tom poked his head into the room, his dark eyes filled with concern. "Groceries are all put away." He stepped toward his wife. "Why don't you lie down for a rest if you're done in here?"

"Oh, Tom, I don't know if I can. I've so much to do before the guests arrive." Betty wrung her hands. "My list of last-minute things to get together for the workshops is a mile long." She looked around at the scattered papers. "And now I have this mess to deal with." Tears formed in her eyes.

"You'll have to leave this untouched until we can go over it." Grayson smoothed a hand over his bald spot.

Tom wrapped his arms around Betty, his large frame enveloping her. "A short rest will do you good." He led her out of the room. Normally a gregarious man, especially around guests, Tom now displayed a much softer, caring side. No wonder their marriage had lasted more than thirty years.

The chief waited to talk to Shannon until Betty and Tom had left the room. "So you think he took something?"

"I think he put something either in a pocket or inside his coat." Shannon surveyed the room. The petty cash lay untouched in an open drawer. A framed set of collector coins hung on the wall, seemingly undisturbed. *What did the thief intend to steal?*

Grayson leaned toward her. "I see your mind racing a hundred miles an hour." He raised his eyebrows in a show of reprimand. "Leave the detective work to my deputies and me."

Shannon sighed. "Sorry." She couldn't help it if her natural curiosity took over. Besides, she wanted to help her friend.

"The one way I *do* want you to help is to tell me if you think you could identify him. I know you said you didn't see his face, but take a moment. Was there anything distinct about the guy?"

"He had a hood on, and he kept his head bent down the whole time." She certainly couldn't remember what he looked like when he had charged at her. "However, his cologne smelled really unique. I'd recognize the smell anywhere."

The chief furled his forehead, and the corners of his mouth turned up. "I don't think there has ever been a police lineup based on smell."

Shannon laughed and put her hands over her face. "Sorry—just trying to remember every detail, anything that might help us catch him." The brief exchange of humor lightened the moment for both of them.

The chief hiked up his belt. "You mean anything that would help *the police* catch him?"

"Yes, of course." Shannon smiled innocently.

"I've got a deputy out searching the area. I'll radio him. If he hasn't found anything, he can drive over to dust for prints and process the scene. With all the guests they're expecting, I'm sure Betty and Tom will need to use the office."

Shannon followed Grayson out to the great room. "I'll let you know if I remember anything else that might be helpful."

"Good. I'll have my officer over here as soon as possible." With a clipped nod, Grayson headed out the door.

Shannon listened to the rumble of his SUV as it pulled out of the driveway. When she walked past the sunroom, she noticed Betty, setting out quilt samples.

"Did you decide not to take that nap?"

Betty shook her head. "I still need the fabric samples from your shop and the beads for the class you're going to teach." She spoke at a rapid pace.

"I can bring those by later today." Shannon unfolded a quilted lap blanket and searched for a place to display it. She found herself wanting to offer words of comfort but unsure of what to say. A break-in like this could make Betty fearful it might happen again—Shannon knew from experience.

Betty bustled around the room, placing quilts over chairs and arranging blocks of fabric on a table. She seemed to be dealing with her emotions by staying busy. "I think this room will be a good place to display things," she said. "If people want to set up quilt projects between classes, they can do it here. This area is really conducive to people visiting with one another while they're working on their projects."

"It sounds like you've thought of everything. I'm sure the guests are going to have a wonderful time."

Betty hadn't stopped moving since Shannon entered the room. Now she rearranged the sample quilt blocks for the third time. "Make sure you remind Deborah to call and let me know exactly what she's covering in her classes, will you? Oh, and she promised she'd bring her quilt frame over."

Deborah Waters, Shannon's cook and an expert quilter, had also been her grandmother Victoria's cook and confidant. "I'll remind her, but I'm sure she's on top of all that."

"I can't tell you how much your coming over has helped me." Betty stopped flitting around the room and looked directly at Shannon, her blue eyes shining with gratitude.

"I'm glad to do it."

"My only sister died when I was young. I can't help but think that if she had lived, she would have been a lot like you." Betty's voice was thick with emotion.

The compliment floored Shannon. "I'm so honored you said that."

"I know you must have a ton of things to do at the craft market, but you chose to help me instead. That means a lot to me."

The decision to help Betty prepare the inn for the workshops had meant work would pile up at Shannon's shop. But it had been worth it to spend time with Betty. Essie Engleman, the manager of the Paisley Craft Market & Artist Lofts, could handle most of the tasks at the shop, and Shannon had hired a high school girl, Kristin O'Connor, to help out during the busy festival. "It was my pleasure. I just wish I could've caught that guy. I think he probably saw the two of you leave and assumed no one occupied that side of the inn."

Outside, the mail truck rumbled all the way up the long driveway.

"He must be bringing a package." Betty hurried across the room. "Probably the special preserves I ordered to serve at breakfast in the tearoom."

Shannon followed behind. Betty opened the door and disappeared outside. She returned with a box a moment later.

Shannon stared at the huge box. "How much jam did you order?"

"Not this much," Betty said. "This is too big to be six jars of marmalade."

Shannon retrieved scissors from the sunroom and handed them to Betty.

Betty checked the sides and the bottom of the box. "Strange. There's no return address."

The beat-up package didn't look like it had been wrapped by a business. Betty cut through the tape, folded the top flaps of the box down, and removed the tissue paper. With a gasp, she took a step back. "How could it be?" she whispered.

Shannon leaned forward and looked down at the folded quilt in the box. Betty's reaction told her it wasn't a sample quilt for the workshops.

Betty drew the quilt out of the box, revealing another quilt beneath it. She held it to her chest, the look of shock on her face even more intense than when she'd learned of the robbery.

"Betty?"

Betty didn't respond. A faraway look formed in the older woman's eyes, now rimmed with tears.

Shannon smoothed her hand over the second quilt still in the box and said, "These hand-stitched quilts are beautiful." She cast a curious glance at Betty. "I wonder who sent them."

The question seemed to snap Betty out of her trance. She tossed the quilt into the box and wiped at the corner of her eyes. "It doesn't matter."

"But you *do* know who they came from."

"This doesn't make any sense," Betty muttered. She picked up the box and dropped it carelessly by the fireplace. Without another word, she disappeared down the hallway.

Confused by her friend's odd behavior, Shannon listened to the hushed voices as Betty talked to Tom. Then she heard what sounded like crying.

Shannon kneeled down and picked up the quilts where Betty had tossed them. She folded the top quilt and carefully placed it in the box. Whoever made the quilts had demonstrated great skill. The quilter had created a pattern of two big stitches and one short stitch, so evenly done that it looked like machine work, though no machine could do that. The quilter had also incorporated bits of lace and embroidery into her pattern.

Shannon didn't know who the quilts might be from—or why Betty had reacted to them so strongly. But she understood one thing for sure: The arrival of the quilts had upset Betty far more than the break-in.